My Wanderlust Bites the Dust

The Travel Mishaps of Caity Shaw
Book Four

Eliza Watson

My Wanderlust Bites the Dust

ISBN-10: 0-9992168-4-8
ISBN-13: 978-0-9992168-4-2

Printed in the United States of America.

BOOKS BY ELIZA WATSON

The Travel Mishaps of Caity Shaw Series

Flying by the Seat of My Knickers (Book 1)

Up the Seine Without a Paddle (Book 2)

My Christmas Goose Is Almost Cooked (Book 3)

My Wanderlust Bites the Dust (Book 4)

Other Books

Kissing My Old Life Au Revoir

Writing Romance as Eliza Watson & Eliza Daly

Under Her Spell

Identity Crisis

'Til Death Do Us Part—Eliza Daly

Writing Young Adult as Beth Watson

Getting a Life, Even If You're Dead

To my dad, Doug Watson, for inspiring my wanderlust.
I will forever cherish the memories of our travels
around the world. I love you.

&

In memory of our 18-year-old kitty, Quigley.
You were my best friend and confidant.
You are deeply missed and loved.

ACKNOWLEDGMENTS

I would like to thank my mom and dad for encouraging me to follow my dream of studying abroad and traveling the world. For the numerous trips we have enjoyed together over the years, including the first visit to our ancestors' homeland, Ireland. It wouldn't have been nearly as special without you both. I'm looking forward to Scotland and walking in the steps of our Watson ancestors!

Thank you to my husband, Mark, and all my friends and family for believing in me and supporting my writing in so many ways. I would have given up years ago without your encouragement. To Nikki Ford, Elizabeth Wright, and Meghan Lloyd for reading this book several times and for your in-depth feedback, helping to make it a stronger book. To Judy Watson for reading the book even after I sent the wrong version. Sorry about that. And to Laura Iding for all the brainstorming and support sessions over wine and dinner.

To Dori Harrell for your fab editorial skills and for always exceeding my expectations. To Chrissy Wolfe for your final proofreading tweaks. Thanks to you ladies I can always publish a book with confidence. To Lyndsey Lewellen for another incredible cover and for capturing the spirit of Caity. And to Amy Atwell at Author E.M.S. for a flawless interior format and for always promptly answering my many questions.

Thanks to my brilliant fans, who began this adventure with Caity in *Flying by the Seat of My Knickers* and who continue to follow her journey around Europe!

My Coffey Family Tree

Cheat Sheet

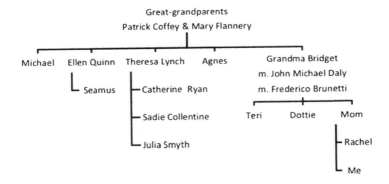

Great-grandparents
Patrick Coffey & Mary Flannery

Michael   Ellen Quinn   Theresa Lynch   Agnes   Grandma Bridget
                                                m. John Michael Daly
          └ Seamus   ┌ Catherine Ryan   m. Frederico Brunetti

                        ├ Sadie Collentine   Teri   Dottie   Mom

                        └ Julia Smyth   ├ Rachel

                                                               └ Me

CHAPTER
ONE

This was going to be the best Valentine's Day since my third-grade crush, Tommy Blanchard, gave me a heart-shaped Play-Doh cookie. I'd cracked a tooth biting into it, expecting a sugar cookie. Sixteen years later, I'd be celebrating the romantic holiday in the fairy-tale city of Prague with the Irish love of my life, Declan. We hadn't seen each other since Christmas in Ireland.

Since the first time we'd said *I love you.*

The thought of experiencing another first together in Prague about made me faint.

I walked through the upscale restaurant searching out the perfect table for our romantic dinner tomorrow night, Valentine's Day Eve. Patrons weren't paying for the basic black-and-white linens and décor—they were paying for the view. I fished my phone from my purse to send Declan a teaser pic from an intimate corner table overlooking the Vltava River. Perched high on a hill, Prague Castle was set against purplish-pink fluffy clouds. I snapped a pic as a text alert shrilled. My hand jerked, causing a blurred picture.

It was from Blair, the meeting's planner.

F & B lead here soon. Come to staff office.

I replied, *On my way!*

The F & B team was in charge of the meeting's food and beverage functions. It wasn't my area of expertise. I didn't have an area of expertise. I also didn't have experience with a group as large as two hundred attendees. Fifty had been my max. And Declan or my sister, Rachel, had always been on-site to have my back. I gave myself a little pep talk to calm the nervous fluttering in my tummy.

I tossed my phone into my purse. I'd missed a shot of the perfect sunset and now didn't have time to shower. I felt skanky, having landed only two hours earlier. It was 4:00 p.m., and my workday was just beginning even though I'd left Milwaukee twenty-two hours ago.

I thanked the host for allowing me a sneak peek at the restaurant and slipped him 400 korunas—twenty bucks—requesting the corner table for the following evening. He gave me an efficient nod. I'd already forked out 500 korunas to my meeting hotel's concierge to secure the last-minute reservation. Declan and I would have to share an appetizer, skip dessert, and drink the house red. But the dinner wouldn't be about the food— it'd be about setting the tone for an evening we'd never forget.

Only nineteen hours until Declan arrived, making a side trip on his way from the Canary Islands to a meeting in Florence.

I let out a contented sigh, and my cheeks flushed from anticipation as I stepped outside into a cool breeze. I envisioned Declan and me strolling hand in hand down the quaint tree-lined cobblestone sidewalk along the river.

A silver-and-red electric tram rolled past. The modern invention was a contrast to the Gothic-style Charles Bridge with its massive stone statues spanning across the river toward the castle. Prague was often referred to as turn-of-the-century Paris. A step back in time. Hopefully I was able to find *time* to step across the bridge and visit my third castle. According to the agenda, no off-site dinners were planned, so we should have some free evenings. I snapped a few pics just in case.

Ten minutes later, I skirted around a tour group outside La Haute Bohème and entered the hotel. An iron railing with decorative brass accents led up the sweeping red-carpeted staircase to the mezzanine level. Etched stained-glass mirrors and art nouveau paintings hung on the walls. Couples decked out in formal attire, likely off to a romantic dinner before attending the opera or symphony, strolled across the white-and-black tiled floor. Feeling out of place in my wrinkled jeans, windblown auburn hair, and no makeup, I imagined myself in a red velvet dress with long satin gloves, like a character on *Downton Abbey*—

"I requested a room on a lower floor." A woman's harsh, demanding voice shattered the ambiance.

An annoyingly familiar voice...

My gaze darted to the blond American arguing with a front desk clerk.

Gretchen!

I gasped, inhaling the mint in my mouth. It shot down my throat too quickly to cause coughing or choking. Yet panic pressed against the lump in my chest. I pounded a fist against my chest, hoping the mint hadn't become lodged in a lung.

Gretchen and I'd met on my first meeting in Dublin. My sister, Rachel, an event planner, thought her star contractor could do no wrong. Even when I'd proved she *could*, defending myself when Gretchen attempted to use me as a scapegoat, Rachel had sided with her. Gretchen had spent the entire meeting making me feel incompetent and causing Rachel to question my abilities, at a time when I was trying to gain my sister's respect and rebuild our relationship.

Also, Gretchen had slept with Declan, once.

I hadn't yet slept with Declan.

"What if there's a fire?" Gretchen said. "I'm not racing down fifteen flights of stairs."

"There's a fire?" called out an alarmed woman from the line forming behind Gretchen.

The front desk clerk peered over at the guest. "I assure you, there is not a fire." He glared at Gretchen, his fingers lashing out at the keyboard, rather than around her neck. He gave her a room key and a strained smile. "Here, madam. It is on the *second* floor."

Gretchen snatched the key from his hand. "Thank you." She spun around, flipping her blond hair over her shoulder, her green-eyed gaze landing on me.

I stifled a distressed squeal, heart thumping against the mint in my chest. She didn't look as shocked to see me as I was to see her.

Her skinny jeans and formfitting black sweater weren't practical for a long flight and preventing a pulmonary embolism. Her jade-colored eye shadow and black winged liner weren't even smudged. I touched my mouth, wishing I'd at least put balm on my dried lips.

She headed toward me, designer suitcase in tow. "Well, hello, Caity. How nice we'll be working together again." Her voice oozed sarcasm.

I plastered on what was likely my fakest smile ever, resembling Gretchen's. "You're here for the Evans and Walker meeting?" The company made high-end desserts and confections, which they distributed in their boutique shops and upscale food halls throughout Europe and the US.

She nodded. "I contacted Nigel, the banquet captain, and asked him to meet us in the staff office so we can inventory the products. There'll be a ton." Her gaze narrowed. "I hope you've worked more F and B functions since Powerscourt in Ireland."

Gretchen was the food and beverage lead?

I was going to be her bitch?

My stomach took a swan dive.

"Yeah, I've worked several," I lied.

Gretchen arched a skeptical brow.

She'd make sure I failed at my job, which wouldn't be difficult, even though I was a bit more experienced than the last time we'd worked together. I couldn't let her shake my confidence. And if she outed me to Blair, that my résumé was embellished, she'd jeopardize her relationship with Rachel, who gave her a ton of work. Yet if she discovered my personal relationship with

Declan, she'd throw me under the bus, or an electric tram, in a heartbeat.

The concierge—a dapper-looking older gentleman in a black suit—stopped as he was passing by. His name tag read *Tobias, Austria*. "The restaurant was to your liking for a romantic dinner?"

Gretchen tilted her head, eying me with curiosity.

I smiled calmly at the man while panic raced through me. "Yes, thank you. It should work out perfectly for them."

His gaze narrowed. "I thought it was—"

"Ideal for my friend's honeymoon this summer? You were right."

The poor man looked confused, since I'd tipped him well to secure a last-minute reservation for me at the city's most romantic restaurant.

I slipped a 500-koruna bill, the smallest I had, from my pocket and handed it to him. Gag money. "Thank you again so much." I'd blown through 1,400 korunas in under an hour. Forget dessert. Declan and I would be sharing a glass of house wine at our romantic table for two.

The concierge walked away with a baffled expression, slipping the money into his pants pocket.

I gave my head a concerned shake. "Hopefully, we won't have to rely on him for too much assistance during our stay."

Hopefully, *I* wouldn't need to rely on him for help, since he now thought I was completely bonkers.

Gretchen looked more annoyed than curious. "Whatever. See you in the office." She strutted off, suitcase bouncing in rhythm with her size D boobs, attracting the attention of several leering businessmen.

Gretchen hadn't even been here five minutes and I'd almost been busted. Declan and I had been discreet about our relationship, never mentioning it on social media. We'd have to continue flying under the radar when he was here. If Gretchen found out I was seeing Declan, she'd make my job an even bigger living hell.

Suddenly, working with two hundred people didn't worry me nearly as much as working with one. Gretchen.

CHAPTER
TWO

I frantically texted Declan on my way to the staff office.
Gretchen is here!

Had he known she was working this meeting? He and Gretchen shared a lot of the same clients, most of whom I'd submitted my résumé to. She and I would likely be working together in the future. I had to figure out a way to tolerate her.

My fingers tightened around the phone. Inhaling a calming breath, I loosened my grip. No way was I allowing that wretched woman to ruin my one romantic evening with Declan.

He replied to my text. *Boarding the group on a boat. Will ring ya soon.*

He'd been warned.

I entered the staff office, smiling at a half dozen unfamiliar faces. My heart thumped wildly, being the new kid on the block. A girl my age—twenty-four—sat at a back table, her fingers pounding her laptop's keyboard, a tear rolling down her cheek, leaving a faint trail of mascara. She looked ready to pull out her short blond hair. Everyone appeared to be ignoring the fact that she was in meltdown mode. Maybe she had a history of being a drama queen. I hoped that was the case and not a sign that I should turn around and run.

I assumed the only person in a black suit, rather than jeans, was Blair, who worked for Taylor Made Events, hired by Evans and Walker to plan their meetings. Her features were all hard angles—high cheekbones, narrow chin, and pointed nose. Her black bob haircut and deep-maroon-colored lips contrasted with her pale skin, even lighter than mine. Her lips clashed with the client's uniform shirt—a pink oxford with an *E & W* in the middle of an embroidered chocolate. Blair carried on an intense conversation with a hotel employee, never glancing my way.

Three staff sat at gold-skirted tables with their backs to a view of a cream-colored building with fancy peach scrollwork and decorative statues. Before I could introduce myself, Gretchen blew in, flitting around, distributing hugs and kisses, droning on about the last time she'd worked with everyone. They appeared happy to see her, putting me at a serious disadvantage.

Mindy, thirtyish with short, dark hair, blue eyes, and a friendly smile, was the VIP lead. Chad comprised the meeting rooms' "team." With his dark tan, it was difficult to determine his age, thirty, maybe forty. He had on jeans and an eggplant-colored paisley print oxford that made me crave my favorite angel-hair pasta dish with eggplant and roasted tomatoes. Rita, a white-haired English woman with a pair of red funky-patterned reading glasses perched on the tip of her nose, was working registration.

"Why isn't Declan here this year?" Chad asked.

I opened my mouth to reply, then snapped it shut when everyone looked at Gretchen for an answer.

"He was already booked for Florence. Will have much better weather, I'm sure."

How did she know Declan would be in Florence? Had he been booked on the meeting when they'd worked in Dublin or Greece last fall? He hadn't posted it on Facebook, and she wouldn't have access to his Google calendar, like I did. Unless she'd hacked into it. I doubted she was that computer savvy. However, she was that *psycho*.

"You ever worked with Declan?" Mindy asked me.

"Ah, yeah, he's great."

Gretchen gave me the evil eye. When Declan and I'd worked together in Dublin, we hadn't been overly friendly, yet Gretchen's claws had come out every time we'd even talked. Not only did I need to make sure *Gretchen* didn't see Declan here, but the entire *staff*, since they'd be sure to mention it.

"Last time I worked with Declan was in Berlin," Chad said. "I just watched a Jason Bourne movie filmed there. You know you travel too much when you start recognizing hotel lobbies, airport terminals, and train stations in movies."

"Hopefully, nobody recognizes this hotel from *Ghost Hunters International*," Mindy said. "It was on the show six months ago."

"This hotel is haunted?" The hairs on my arms shot up.

Chad nodded. "Supposedly one of the most haunted in the world."

Gretchen rolled her eyes. "If you believe in that stuff."

I wasn't sure if I believed in ghosts. The fact that Gretchen didn't believe made me want to believe all the more. Declan had once told me that believing there's something more after death was the only thing that helped him live with a loss. I hadn't known at the time he was referring to his wife.

"Why is it haunted?" I asked.

"It's not, as far as we're concerned," Blair snapped, joining our conversation. "We chose this place because we got a great group rate and we fit the meeting space. Don't discuss its haunted history in or out of the office."

"The ghost tour groups in front of the hotel every night might give it away," Chad said.

That was a *ghost* tour out front?

"It just better not come from us," Blair said.

Everyone agreed mum was the word and returned to work.

Blair eyed me. "So, Caity, Gretchen mentioned you guys have worked together before. That your sister is a planner for Brecker beer."

Great. She'd probably told Blair I'd gotten the job thanks to nepotism rather than being qualified. Which I had.

"She is, but I have a lot of other clients..." I trailed off as Blair tapped a long, maroon-polished nail impatiently against her cell phone.

"Thanks so much for fitting this meeting in after all," she told Gretchen. "I put the product inventory list with the BEOs on your guys' desk." Blair left the conversation as abruptly as she'd joined it. She had a brief discussion with the girl melting down, who shot Blair a nasty look as she walked over to her desk. It apparently hadn't been a pep talk.

The poor thing. I'd had my share of breakdowns onsite.

Gretchen snatched the inventory list off her desk. "The banquet captain will take us to the locked cooler so we can verify if all the product is here." She scanned the items. "One hundred packages of Kittridge, two hundred Ethan Hunt..."

"Those are names from *Mission Impossible*." I'd watched the movie set in Prague before coming.

"Everything has code names. This is a new product-launch tasting, so items aren't yet available at retailers."

I knew that from the advance communication.

"We have to account for every piece of product and know its whereabouts at all times. We're responsible for getting items to the meeting rooms and making sure any remaining ones are destroyed. The client's security team will help with that. They'll be stationed at every food function to prevent corporate espionage."

This sounded like a James Bond movie and way above my pay grade.

My phone rang. I pulled it from my purse to find Declan's number. I accepted the call without thinking, then snapped the phone against my chest so he wasn't visible. Thankfully, Gretchen was focused on the inventory list, not my caller.

"I have to take this."

Her brows furrowed into a peeved look. "Don't be

long. We need to get this inventory done in case we have to track down missing items or replace pilfered ones."

I flew into the foyer, drawing the phone back from my chest.

"Brilliant view," Declan said, a mischievous glint in his eyes. "Should I have rang ya from my guest room?"

"Ha-ha."

I stepped out a side door into pedestrian traffic and honking cars. My teeth chattered, whereas Declan's skin looked sun kissed. Behind him, attendees were bobbing along on top of a blue sea, snorkeling. The wind whipped my hair against my face, and I yanked it back behind my ear. Not a strand of Declan's wavy, short brown hair was out of place.

"Looks nice there."

"A bit cool, but the group's from Norway. How's it going with Gretchen? When I'd mentioned last fall I wasn't working this meeting, she said she wasn't either. That she was fed up with Blair's attitude."

"Yeah, Blair seems a bit intense."

He shrugged. "Take her with a grain of salt. Same as Gretchen. Don't let her rattle you. You'll be grand."

"We can't let her find out you're going to be here. We have to be discreet. I'll leave a key in an envelope for you at the front desk since I can't put your name on the room. I also shouldn't put your name on the envelope. I'll put it under... What's your middle name?"

"Colin."

His dad's name. Declan's family lived a half hour from my grandma Coffey Brunetti's long-lost rellies in Ireland's Midlands. I'd visited the area at Christmas. Because of canceled flights, I'd spent Christmas Eve with

Declan's family and had flown home Christmas Day.

"Okay, I'll put it under Colin Grady."

He quirked a brow, wearing a sly smile. "Feels a bit like a forbidden liaison. No worries. I'll be discreet. Wouldn't want Blair to find out either, since staff aren't allowed to have guests."

"Why didn't you tell me that?"

I desperately needed future business from Blair. I still had a major credit card to pay off, my student loan kicked in next month, and self-employment taxes were looming in my future. I only had two meetings on the books and a pending bonus from Brecker for helping to get Brecker Dark into Finn O'Brien's restaurant chain business in Ireland. The restaurants had only carried a cider ale manufactured by Flanagan's—an Irish beer company owned by Brecker. Choking—actually gagging—on the chef's goose curry had paid off. How much, I didn't yet know.

"Because you might have told me not to come," he said.

"I'd never have told you that." I gave him a flirty smile. "You're worth the risk. And I have a surprise planned."

When we'd said "I love you" for the first time at Grandma's childhood home in Ireland, I'd promised myself I'd never let anything come between us. Not even my job. Yet my job was the only way we were able to see each other.

Talk about a double-edged sword.

∂✽ ✿∂

After standing outside freezing, I was shivering inside the hotel's cooler, a black table linen wrapped around my shoulders. Actually, the Evans and Walker product Gretchen and I were inventorying was secured in a padlocked iron-bar cage within the walk-in refrigerator. I wasn't sure if it was the dim lighting, my feeling of impending doom, or having been confined in an airplane forever, but the bars suddenly seemed to be closing in. It could also be that I was up to my waist in boxes labeled *Confidential*, barely able to move.

My gaze darted to the outer door. What if it had locked behind us? The thought of being imprisoned with the nastiest cellmate ever caused my heart to race, my breathing to quicken. I snapped a hand against my chest, realizing the lump from the mint was gone.

One problem solved.

Gretchen had on a black wool jacket, knowing we'd be in a cooler. She glanced up from counting the product labeled with the code name *Ethan Hunt* in black letters on generic silver packaging. She gave me an impatient look. "Are you okay?"

I nodded. "It's dark in here." I squinted at the inventory list in my numb hand. "Isn't it dark in here? Maybe I should open a door." Before I tunneled my way out of the fridge to the Charles Bridge.

I escaped from the unlocked cage and pushed open the cooler's heavy door. I stepped out into the bright, shiny stainless-steel kitchen, sucking in some serious air, welcoming the stench of greasy food and burned coffee. I eased out a breath.

The last time I'd had this panicked feeling, I'd been

visiting the Catacombs in Paris, 130 steps below ground with six million dead people.

A server in a black suit—tall, blond, fortyish—eyed the tablecloth wrapped around me. His name tag read *Oscar, Sweden*. "Are you okay? Would you like another linen?"

"No, I'm good." I gave him a reassuring smile.

"You know, it'd be really great to finish this inventorying before midnight so I could get at least five hours of sleep." Gretchen stood glaring at me, in her hand the butcher knife she was using to slice open boxes.

Oscar bolted.

It'd be really *super* if I didn't hyperventilate and pass out and wake up to find Gretchen or Oscar giving me mouth-to-mouth.

I propped open the cooler's door with a case of bottled water and reluctantly returned to our cell. I focused on the light and the activity pouring in from the kitchen, rather than the suffocating tension inside the cage. *Don't let her rattle you. You'll be grand.* I repeated Declan's pep talk in my head, glancing around at the bars, trying to find humor in the fact that I shouldn't let Gretchen *rattle my cage.*

I was still freezing when I got to my room at 10:00 p.m.

Only thirteen hours until Declan landed.

Thankfully, Blair reconfirmed we'd have off tomorrow night.

I needed to make sure I didn't deplete my entire cash reserve before dinner.

Having been up over thirty hours, I glared at my purple floral suitcase and brown leather carry-on, too exhausted to unpack. I dropped my computer bag on a gold velvet chair. I kicked off my shoes but kept on my green cardigan. I snagged the plush white velour robe from the closet and wrapped myself in it. Declan would have a fit that I was snuggled up in the garment that rarely saw the wash, and that I wasn't removing the dodgy duvet from the four-poster bed. Right now, I was more likely to catch pneumonia than contract something from the bed linens and robe.

Smiling at the thought of Declan's travel quirks, I slipped the TV remote inside a plastic baggie and sanitized the glasses with a bottle of duty-free whiskey I'd bought Declan, wanting him to feel at home. I'd wipe the bathroom and phones down with antibacterial wipes later.

I cranked up the heat and made a hot cup of decaffeinated Barry's Gold. A store in Milwaukee carried the Irish tea, so I no longer had to stock up when I was in Ireland. I cradled the warm mug in my hands, the feeling slowly returning to my fingers. I sat on the crisp white sheets enclosing a soft fleece blanket and rested my back against the headboard. I set the mug on the nightstand next to the 1930s framed photo of Grandma and her sister Theresa, dressed in cloche hats and calf-length dresses made of flowing fabric. They stood in front of the church in Killybog, where I'd attended Mass with Declan and his parents at Christmastime.

I perched my computer on my lap and scanned e-mails, surprised it'd been almost ten hours since I'd received one from Mom. Bernice and Gracie had sent their daily e-mail, checking my progress on their ancestry research.

The two elderly women from my Dublin Christmas meeting had hired me to research their McKinney family before their summer trip to Scotland. I'd warned them I wouldn't have time to work on it while traveling. I needed to spend my free hours eating and sleeping. And they'd known when they'd hired me I was far from competent. I hadn't even had an Ancestry.com subscription. This past month, I'd spent dozens of hours learning to navigate the research site. I still wasn't proficient at finding information. No way would I have time to research my Flannery family and find living rellies before my St. Paddy's Day meeting in Dublin.

The subject of the next e-mail read *New Message from George on Bridget Coffey*. Finally. After four months, my first response from a message I'd posted on an Ireland genealogy forum.

I opened the e-mail.

Hello Ms. Shaw,

I read on this forum that you are researching a Bridget Coffey from Killybog, County Westmeath, Ireland. I am wondering if perhaps this is the same Bridget Coffey who married John Michael Daly in Lancashire, England. If yes, or you believe it could be,

I would be quite interested in communicating with you
and sharing information.
Kind regards,
George Wood

It was indeed the same Bridget Coffey. John Michael Daly had been her first husband. A husband my family had no clue about until recently, years after Grandma's death. I'd tracked down John Daly's sister, Emily, in Ireland at Christmas, thanks to the help of Grandma's newfound niece, Sadie Collentine. Emily had confirmed Grandma and her first husband had lived in Lancashire after becoming estranged from their families in Ireland. Their families' feud was deeply rooted in the fact that the Dalys had owned the land Grandma's family had farmed for generations. Two years after marrying, John Michael died from TB. Grandma returned briefly to Ireland before immigrating to America.

Was George Wood related to Grandma or the Dalys? Did he know where she and John Michael had lived in England? The church where their forbidden marriage had taken place?

Excitement zipped through me. Any information this George could provide would be more than what we knew about Grandma's life in England. We still knew little about her life in Ireland.

CHAPTER THREE

My day started with a grueling two-hour food and beverage meeting with Gretchen and Nigel, the banquet captain. I scribbled Gretchen's changes on the event orders, hoping I'd be able to decipher them later, and highlighted critical notes in green. She provided the exact number of coffee and tea gallons for every meal function. Made changes to every room setup diagram. Reiterated a dozen times that the product cage must remain locked at all times and only Nigel and she were to have keys. And anyone found accessing the product without permission would be guillotined in Prague's Old Town Square when the astronomical clock struck midnight. She didn't say that, but it was inferred.

I was breaking out in a sweat, gulping down bottled sparkling water, which I despised. However, Nigel remained unflappable.

"Please don't worry," Nigel said in a refined English accent. His tailored black suit and crisp white shirt matched his demeanor. "I assure you the meeting will be impeccably executed."

The word "executed" and visions of a guillotine made me cringe.

"I'm sure it will." Gretchen smiled sweetly, though a warning look flashed in her green eyes, enhanced with her usual jade eye shadow and winged liquid liner. She must get up an hour early just to do her eyes.

She abruptly stood and left.

We were dismissed.

I released my grip on the gold hotel pen and massaged the cramp from my hand. My black suit jacket draped on the chair back was wrinkled from my rigid body pressing against it for hours. I slipped it on over my pink button-up oxford with an *E & W* swirled chocolate logo. I swiped magenta lip gloss across my lips and smoothed a hand over my flat-ironed auburn hair. If Declan wasn't coming today, I'd have just tossed my hair up in a clip and slept an extra half hour. I straightened my pile of event orders, glancing over at Nigel.

"She can be a bit overwhelming, but she knows her stuff. She's a food and beverage goddess."

Had I seriously just referred to Gretchen as a *goddess*? Yet I didn't have to like her to learn from her. Maybe Rachel couldn't stand her personally either but relied on her professional expertise to run a successful meeting, same as Blair appeared to. A lot of the revisions and information Gretchen had provided Nigel seemed like stuff Blair should have planned in advance.

Nigel gave me a polite smile. "Yes. She appears quite competent at her job, as am I. I'm sure we'll do just fine."

Oh, to have his confidence.

On my way back to the office, I received a text from Declan that put a bounce in my step.

Just landed. Can't wait to see you!

I wiped the goofy grin off my face when I entered the office, not wanting my cheerful attitude to arouse suspicion.

The girl in the corner was slamming a Red Bull energy drink. She tore a report to shreds and tossed it in the garbage. I'd learned her name was Courtney. She'd taken over the meeting's registration process last week after her coworker had quit without notice because of a nasty confrontation with Blair. She'd gone out with a bang—sabotaging the registration database. Now, it was Courtney's job to fix it. Everyone was holding their breath that she didn't bolt before the meeting even started.

I sat next to Gretchen typing away on her laptop. Blair marched up with an intense look, her deep-maroon lips pressed into a sliver. I sat at attention, pen poised, preparing for whatever she was about to throw at me. Mindy trailed behind her with pink lips and sparkly pink earrings, both of which matched the uniform shirt to a tee. She'd obviously done several Evans and Walker meetings. Since I hadn't, all my jewelry was boring black or silver so it would go with any color.

"I need you to help Mindy check VIP suites. We just got the keys and were given the former Bridal Suite when we specifically forbid it from being included in our room block. The contracted suite is occupied and won't be vacated before Mr. Gauthier arrives." Blair glanced around, then lowered her voice. "I don't believe in ghosts, but I don't need to have a VIP go off on me because we put him in a room where someone was killed eighty years ago."

Killed? I didn't dare ask how, since Blair looked like somebody was on *her* hit list, her hands clenched into fists. Even if I didn't believe in ghosts, someone having died, possibly been murdered in the suite, was totally creepy. No way would I sleep in that room.

Blair relaxed her fists, her long nails leaving deep impressions in her palms. "Just one more '*challenge*'"—she made air quotes—"to deal with. Make sure the hotel's haunted history channel isn't on the TVs. Even though it's now called the Presidential Suite, and the black-and-white photos are from the 1930s, it'd be just my luck the guy would recognize it as his room." She glanced over at me. "I'll run you off a suite checklist."

"I have one." Rachel had given me a two-page list when I'd helped her check a suite my first meeting in Dublin.

"I'd prefer you use mine," Blair said. "And make sure they've swapped out the minibar items with Evans and Walker products. Ones that are already in stores."

No way would her list be more thorough than Rachel's, which I'd take with me anyway. This was my moment to shine. Rachel had taught me to look for everything from a handprint on a window to undies in nightstands. As long as I didn't have to wear a proton pack strapped to my back to hunt ghosts, I'd be fine.

Mindy and I entered the former Bridal Suite. We peered cautiously around at the sunny-yellow room filled with gilded framed artwork and mirrors and gold velvet furnishings with red decorative pillows. I pictured an elegantly dressed woman with a long cigarette holder lounging on the fainting couch in the corner, her husband sitting in the gold high-back chair, drinking a scotch while reading an article about prohibition in America. A black iron spiral staircase with decorative spindles led to an upper floor.

A door slammed down the hallway.

Mindy let out a startled gasp, her gaze darting to the suite's door. "Ah, this place is four times bigger than the other three suites. I can check those in the time it'll take you to check this one. Let's divide and conquer." She slapped the room key in my hand and vanished out the door.

Silence filled the air. No noise from neighbors. No heat kicking in. No fridge humming. It was eerily quiet. Goose bumps skittered across my skin. *Get a grip.* Again, I'd survived the Catacombs in Paris. I was not letting a brightly decorated room, eight stories *above* ground, freak me out.

I pressed the TV remote's On button. The screen remained black. I clicked it repeatedly. Still nada. The goose bumps were back. I assured myself it just needed a new battery. It wasn't like a ghost was preventing me from having the haunted history channel removed. When the master bedroom's TV turned on, I let out a relieved sigh. *Welcome to La Haute Bohème* filled the screen, followed by scenes of the hotel's luxurious spa and elegant restaurants. No ghost pics or scary story.

I'd rather not know how the person had been killed. And if it was one of the most haunted hotels in the world, it seemed likely there had to be more than one resident ghost. Either that or the ghost in this room was super busy.

A text dinged on my phone, about launching me into the air.

I'm here.

Rather than a ghost communicating via text, it was Declan.

Gonna run and get a bite.

My shoulders sagged in disappointment even though there would be no such thing as a quick hello when we hadn't seen each other in fifty days. It would make tonight even more special.

Smiling, I typed, *Checking the Presidential Suite. See you at 7.*

I noted *TV remote batteries* on the list of items for the hotel to address. I finished inspecting the living room, flipping over a stained gold chair cushion and straightening magazines on a glass-topped cocktail table. I opened a door off the entryway, surprised to find a bathroom rather than a closet. I flushed the toilet to make sure it worked, and the porcelain tank fell against the wall. Crap. Yet at least I'd found something to be fixed, or Blair would think I was incompetent.

I was counting the closet hangers in the master bedroom when a pounding sound came from the living room. My heart thumped. I stepped cautiously from the walk-in closet, and the noise grew louder. Someone was knocking on the front door. Housekeeping? I crept over and peeked through the peephole.

Nobody was there.

The hairs on my arms shot up.

The knock sounded again, followed by, "Caity?"

Declan? Heart racing, I opened the door.

He gave me a sly smile, his blue eyes twinkling. "Only one Presidential Suite in the hotel."

He glanced up and down the hallway. Coast clear, he slipped inside the room, closing the door behind him. He wrapped his arms around my waist, pulling me snuggly against him. I curled my fingers into his soft blue wool sweater. I inhaled his rain-scented shampoo and musky cologne as we both went in for a kiss. We were all over each other. Like we hadn't been together in fifty days. Wrapped in each other's arms, we stumbled back against the couch, nearly tumbling onto it.

My phone shrilled.

For the love of God!

We reluctantly peeled ourselves from each other, breathing heavily. I slipped the phone from my jacket pocket. Mindy.

Is my clipboard there?

Her pink clipboard sat on the credenza.

Yes.

K. Be right there.

My gaze darted to Declan. "Mindy is on her way here."

"Right, then. We best hurry." He kissed me with a sense of urgency.

It took every ounce of willpower for me to draw back. "Hold that thought."

As we walked across the mosaic-tiled foyer, a knock sounded at the door. I opened the bathroom door and shoved Declan inside. I greeted Mindy with her clipboard.

"How's it going?" she asked hesitantly, like she'd been expecting me to run screaming from the room.

"Great. Just a few things here and there."

A thud came from inside the bathroom.

Mindy's gaze darted to the bathroom door, whereas I kept mine glued to her.

She peered back at me, looking a tad freaked out. "Did you hear that?"

"What?"

She slowly shook her head. "Ah, nothing. I'll see you back at the office."

She fled, and Declan stepped from the bathroom. "Did you know the toilet is banjacked?"

I nodded. I gave him a fleeting kiss. "Eat a light lunch. We have dinner plans."

A sexy smile curled his lips, like he might have other plans for our evening. The goose bumps were back, but they were good ones this time, not the scary ones.

CHAPTER FOUR

I swiped magenta-colored lip gloss across my lips while waiting for the elevator and tucked stray strands of hair behind my ear. The natural wave had returned to my flat-ironed hair. I'd have no time to restyle it, since our dinner reservation was in a half hour. I impatiently stabbed the elevator button. My abdomen gurgled. I placed a comforting hand against it. Even though I hadn't eaten in eight hours, it wasn't hunger pains. Stress? Exhaustion?

My phone rang.

Rather than Declan checking on my tardiness, it was Blair.

"We just found out Mr. Gauthier hopped on an earlier flight and he's landed. Mindy's checking a suite for a morning arrival. I need you to greet him. I'll run his packet up to you in the lobby." Click.

My grasp tightened around my phone. She'd assured us we'd have off tonight. I wasn't even working VIPs! The elevator doors slid open. I spun around and stalked back toward the lobby. I texted Declan about my delay.

He responded, *Waiting in our room with a surprise.*

My heart rate kicked up a notch, and my mind raced with ideas about his surprise.

Blair arrived with a large white envelope containing Mr. Gauthier's meeting info. A sticky note on the outside had the airport sedan's license plate number. She handed me his room key packet, and I slipped it into my suit jacket pocket.

"I'm in the middle of another *challenge,* or I'd meet him myself. And you speak French, so that's perfect. He'll be impressed. His English isn't very good."

She bolted before I could confess that my French language ability was more conversational than proficient, as my résumé claimed. After composing a few coherent French sentences on my Paris trip last fall, I'd felt a false sense of competency and added it to my résumé.

Ten minutes later, I was pacing the lobby, avoiding the concierge's wary gaze. He needn't worry about me approaching him with some crazy request, unless he spoke French. I was scrambling to string together a few French sentences, preparing for Mr. Gauthier's arrival.

A text alert dinged on my phone in my jacket pocket. Mom.

Did you remember your pepper spray?

Yep, I did.

She shouldn't have a reason to go through my undies drawer and find the defense spray. Not packing it had been a major step forward for me. Eight months after escaping an emotionally abusive relationship, I no longer felt as paranoid that my psycho ex-boyfriend, Andy, might be stalking me. Random smells, sounds, or people's actions reminding me of him were getting rarer and rarer. The only time I'd gone to see Martha, a counselor, in the past two months was to donate hotel toiletries to her women's shelter. I hadn't needed further counseling. I was proud of how far I'd come in a relatively short time, considering what a brainwashed emotional wreck I'd been when Martha had come to my rescue.

I couldn't believe Mom had let me leave the house without the spray. She was obviously becoming more comfortable with me traveling to foreign countries. She'd only contacted me twice today. At Christmas, she'd been forced to have faith that I could survive alone in Ireland. She'd been busy preparing for our annual holiday party and playing nurse to my dad after he'd broken his arm and thrown out his back.

Gretchen strutted through the lobby with Chad. She wore an open black wool jacket, a low-cut slutty green sweater that matched her eyes, jeans, and black spiked heels. "We're off to dinner. Have a great night." She gave me a flutter wave.

Chad nodded, then continued texting on his phone.

How romantic. Just the two of them going to dinner. I'd love for her to know whom *I* was joining for dinner.

Hopefully.

A black sedan pulled up with the license plate number on the sticky note. I darted outside and greeted Mr. Gauthier—fiftyish with salt-and-pepper hair, brown eyes, and olive-toned skin. His power suit was barely wrinkled, and his shoes were buffed to a shine. I escorted him inside and gave him his meeting packet and a brief welcome spiel in broken French with lots of hand gestures. I advised him to supply the front desk with a credit card for expenses. I slipped his key packet from my jacket pocket and handed it to him.

He nodded, appearing to understand. *"Merci."* He headed toward the front desk.

A sense of pride rose inside me, and I breathed a relieved sigh. Yet I made a mental note to remove French language skills from my résumé and to add a translation app to my phone.

Fifteen minutes until our dinner reservation. I called the restaurant, and they reluctantly agreed to hold our table for a half hour.

I placed a hand over my mouth, stifling a yawn, then slapped it against my abdomen. The funky gurgling was back in full force. Not wanting it to ruin our evening, I flew over to the gift shop to grab medicine and an energy drink.

The sales clerk required my key to make a room charge.

I slipped it from my pocket and handed it to her.

Her gaze narrowed on the key packet. "Room 812 does not match your name."

"It's room 642."

She shook her head.

I snatched the packet from her hand. Room 812. The haunted suite. Holy crap. I'd given Mr. Gauthier *my* key packet.

And Declan was waiting in our room for him with a *surprise*.

What if he was sprawled naked across the white sheets, blanketed in rose petals, holding a glass of champagne?

Heart racing, I flew out of the gift shop. I whisked past the front desk. No Mr. Gauthier. I called Declan as I bolted toward the elevators but got his voicemail. I stabbed the elevator button. The door finally opened, and I shot inside without allowing guests to first exit.

How was I going to explain my screwup? Did a hotel ever mistakenly assign the same room to more than one guest? No clue, but that was the story I was going with. Yet that didn't help the awkward encounter likely occurring right now between Declan and Mr. Gauthier. And since Declan had previously worked Evans and Walker meetings, the VIP would likely recognize him!

I exited the elevator and flew down the hallway to my room. I rapped on the door. My heart pounded. Declan greeted me with a relaxed smile.

"Are you alone?" I whispered, peering over his shoulder.

Confusion wrinkled his brow. "Ah, yeah, of course I'm alone."

I let out a relieved sigh, eying his jeans, white button-down shirt, black vest, and black-and-gray tie. "And thank God you're dressed."

He quirked a curious brow. "Right, then. Not quite the reaction I was hoping for tonight."

"Sorry. I just have a minor snafu to take care of. Be right back." I gave him a fleeting kiss. "Make sure you lock the door and keep your clothes on."

"What the hell is going on?" he called after me as I raced down the hallway.

I rode the elevator down, letting out an impatient sigh at each floor it stopped on. I wondered if Mr. Gauthier was on the elevator next to me, heading up. Or maybe he was drinking a scotch in the lounge, or... He'd smelled like cigarettes.

He was probably outside smoking.

Upon reaching the lobby, the elevator doors slid open and I caught a glimpse of Mr. Gauthier entering the elevator across.

"Excuse me," I said, pushing my way through the crush of people to the front.

I exited as Mr. Gauthier's elevator doors started closing. I bolted over and stepped in, the doors slamming against my shoulders and arms, wedging me in place. An older woman in a long purple coat and sparkly diamond rings gasped with surprise, and her small leashed dog yipped. The alarm started ringing. People covered their ears. My heart raced. The dog let out a bark, his butt quivered, and a yellow puddle appeared on the floor, dangerously close to Mr. Gauthier's leather shoes. My eyes widened in horror. Everyone stepped back, including the VIP. The woman scooped up her dog, her nasty look darting between me and the pee puddle.

As if I was in a position to clean it up.

Mr. Gauthier offered her a white hanky with a blue embroidered monogram.

Just shoot me now.

I pressed my shoulder into the door, trying to open it. The concierge rushed up, grasped ahold of a door panel, and pushed it back, freeing me. The ringing stopped, yet continued in my head. I slipped inside,

stepping around the woman cleaning up the puddle
with the VIP's hanky. I turned and thanked the
concierge, who was bent over, hands braced against his
legs, trying to catch his breath. The doors closed, and I
assured everyone I was fine, ignoring the woman and
her dog glaring at me, and the throbbing pain in my
right shoulder, which was going to be a killer bruise.

I smiled cheerfully at Mr. Gauthier, as if nothing had
happened, unsure if I should apologize about his
hanky. Yet a faulty elevator door hadn't been my fault. I
held up the VIP's key packet. Despite being totally
frazzled, I managed to spit out, *"Avez-vous votre clé?"*

He nodded, producing his key. I exchanged our key
packets.

I couldn't even begin to explain the situation in
English, let alone French, so I said, *"C'est un faux
nombre."* It's a false number. Not exactly correct, but
he got my drift. I pressed the button for his floor.

He smiled in understanding, looking appreciative
that I'd risked life and limb to track him down. At least
my mistake had possibly earned me brownie points.
Except for his ruined hanky.

The elderly woman exited on the first stop, giving
Mr. Gauthier an appreciative smile and me the evil eye,
her dog clutched against her chest.

Mr. Gauthier's floor was next. We exchanged *bonsoirs.*

I let out a whoosh of relief, massaging my shoulder
while rotating it in a circular motion. I headed back
down to the gift shop for my medicine. The pink bottle
and energy drink still sat at the clerk's register. I gave
her my correct room key, and she gave me a curious
look. I shrugged. I slammed the energy drink as I

headed across the lobby, then downed two large gulps of the pasty pink liquid as I rode the elevator up.

If Mr. Gauthier mentioned this to Mindy, I'd say I'd checked the key and it had demagnetized, like they always did. That would make me look even more on top of things. Except, then I'd have given him a bad key *before* having checked it...

One issue at a time. I needed to focus on the gurgling in my abdomen that was turning into cramping as I neared my room.

What was the deal? Stress, nerves, exhaustion... Andy?

I slowed my pace. After Andy, I'd worried that I'd never be able to sleep with a guy again. My ex-boyfriend had been controlling both in and out of bed. Sex had always been *when* and *how* he'd wanted. My breathing became labored.

He was nearly out of my *head*, yet not out of my *bed*?

Stop! How could I be thinking about that narcissistic bastard when Declan was waiting in my room for me? I was both physically and mentally prepared to sleep with Declan. I choked down another gulp of medicine and shoved aside thoughts of Andy. I put on a sexy little smile before knocking on the door.

The lock clicked, and Declan appeared.

I eyed his outfit with appreciation, now having time to enjoy the view as I stepped inside. "Very dapper."

"Thanks. Get everything sorted, did ya?"

I nodded. "But no talking work tonight."

Declan knew about my screwups more than anyone. He'd saved my butt and talked me off the ledge numerous times. But I wasn't going to waste the little time we had together bitching about work.

"Ah, right. Maybe we shouldn't talk at all then."

He slipped his arms around my waist and drew me against him. We got hot and heavy, neither of us coming up for air. His hand slipped under my shirt, and his fingers grazed my bare skin, sending tingles up my back, causing faint gurgling in my abdomen.

Declan drew back, smiling. "Starvin', are ya?"

I nodded faintly. "Yeah, we should get to dinner."

"How about some champagne first?" He gestured to two flutes and a bottle chilling in a silver ice bucket on the cocktail table. Was that the surprise he'd mentioned?

"Perfect. But we'll have to slam it."

He quirked a brow. "From the bottle, or can I be putting it in glasses?"

"Either is fine."

I grabbed my black lace shirt and black pants from the closet and flew into the bathroom. I'd hidden my new red silk bra and undies in the shirt sleeve. I quickly changed. My bra straps, and the swollen purplish bruise already forming on my shoulder, were visible beneath the black lace. I swiped on red lip gloss and put on a few fresh coats of black mascara to bring out the blue in my eyes and to appear more wide awake.

"Ooh la la," Declan muttered as I walked out and joined him on the couch. With a steamy look, he traced a gentle finger along my bra strap, opposite shoulder of my bruise.

Gazes locked, we raised our flutes and touched glasses. I took a long sip. I was so thirsty I wanted to chug it, but I also didn't want it to go to my head or upset my tummy, which had calmed down a bit, now cemented with the pasty medicine. I wanted to remember every second of tonight and avoid a hangover. I was worried enough what I'd look like after waking up with Declan for the first time.

Declan reached under the couch and slipped out a red-wrapped box with a gold ribbon.

I eyed the package. "We promised no gifts."

"You're taking me to dinner."

"That's different."

"Just open it."

I slowly unwrapped the box. Rather than a red risqué nightie, a dozen red bags of cheese and onion Taytos—Ireland's yummy potato chips—were laid out in rows. I loved that Declan remembered my obsession with the crisps. That we knew these little things about each other. Something so personal was way better than a silk nightie.

I smiled, relaxing back against Declan's arm draped behind me on the couch. "This is the best present ever."

A text alert shrilled from my cell phone, and my body tensed. Seriously? I snatched the phone from my purse.

Need u to catch cricket in Mr. Gauthier's suite. He just left for dinner. I don't trust hotel to do it.

"What the hell," I muttered. "Blair needs me to find a cricket in a VIP's suite?"

"That's a new one, isn't it?"

"Am I being punked? My initiation as the newbie in the group?"

"I think she's serious."

I sprang from the couch, my grip tightening around the phone. "I am not missing dinner to catch some flippin' cricket. It'll take us forever. The Presidential Suite is huge...and haunted."

I had a strange feeling Mr. Gauthier was going to haunt me more than any ghost on this meeting.

The corners of Declan's mouth curled into an amused smile. "Haunted? Maybe it's not a cricket this bloke's hearing." He waggled his fingers in a mysterious manner. "Or maybe a cricket was murdered in the suite and is now haunting it to drive people mad."

"It's a cricket. It doesn't have to haunt people to drive them mad."

"The only thing I've ever caught in a suite was a keynote speaker shagging a room service guy when I was delivering an amenity, and she hadn't locked her door. She was covered in the hotel's signature chocolate soufflé with cherries strategically placed..."

I smiled faintly yet shook the phone in my hand. "I'm texting her that I'm out to dinner and can't do it." I started frantically typing.

Declan stood and covered my hands with his, preventing my texting. "Take a deep breath."

"But I—"

"Deep breath." He inhaled a lungful of air, and I reluctantly did the same, welcoming the scent of his woodsy cologne. "Now let's go find the sneaky yoke. It's your first meeting with Blair. She won't be hiring you again if you don't."

"I don't care."

"Yes, ya do."

Okay, I did. I was so ticked off about a cricket ruining our romantic dinner it was a good thing Declan was still able to think rationally. He took the service elevator up while I texted Blair and ran to the front desk and got the suite key.

When I joined Declan at the room, he was Googling the hotel's history on his phone. "Did ya know a bride-to-be was killed in this suite?"

I plugged my ears. "La-la-la-la. I don't want to hear a sad or scary story. If I freak myself out, I'll have nightmares or hear chains being dragged across the floor above my room." I unplugged my ears. "Nobody was killed in *my* room, were they?"

Declan shrugged. "Haven't a clue. Should I finish reading the article?"

I shook my head as we stepped inside the suite and turned on a table lamp, dimly lighting the room. We stood quietly in the foyer. No chirp. We went into the master bedroom, leaving off the light.

"It's more likely to chirp in the dark," Declan whispered.

Although ambient light filtered in through the open drapes, the idea of skulking around in a haunted room in the dark raised the hair on the back of my neck.

Chirp.

We froze.

The chirping seemed to be coming from the TV credenza. Declan snagged a to-go cup by the coffee machine and quietly crouched down next to the stand. Several more chirps, and he motioned for me to flip on the light.

The room lit up, yet he couldn't find the cricket.

I got down on my hands and knees and crawled around, helping him search under the furniture. I found a peanut and a wine cork, but no cricket.

Declan pressed his ear to the wall. "Jaysus. It's coming from the next room. Along with an owl hooting. It's a bloody sound machine."

"As if chirping crickets are relaxing?"

The sound certainly wasn't calming *my* nerves.

Declan stayed behind while I knocked on the neighbor's door. Nobody answered. Either the person was sleeping soundly or had left the machine on. I called Blair and explained the culprit was Mr. Gauthier's neighbor. A few minutes later, Blair called and said the hotel solved the *challenge* by upgrading the neighbor to the concierge level. So, all you had to do to get a hotel upgrade was to travel with an annoying sound machine?

I glanced at the time on my phone, groaning in frustration. We'd missed our romantic dinner, and I was out 1,400 korunas for tipping the hotel concierge and restaurant host.

Declan gave me a kiss. "Fancy an absinthe and a bite to eat? I'm sure we can find a lovely café."

I'd never heard of absinthe until our Paris meeting. Declan had described it as a wicked-strong liquor that made artists and writers think they were brilliantly creative when often they'd just gone mad from too much alcohol.

"Although, don't be wanting the liquor to affect my memory of tonight." He cupped my face in his hands and kissed me.

My stomach went berserk. I drew back. "We can't make out in a VIP suite." And with my tummy issues.

Declan smiled, grasping hold of my hand. "Best go before the bloke gets back from dinner."

Yeah, I certainly didn't want Mr. Gauthier to return and find me making out with my boyfriend in his suite. He might assume that was why I'd had his suite key in the first place.

CHAPTER FIVE

Tall, black iron lanterns situated between massive stone statues cast a yellow hue across the Charles Bridge. Prague Castle lit up the evening sky. Despite the cool breeze, I was warm all over as Declan and I strolled hand in hand across the river. I was so caught up in the moment I didn't care if we ran into coworkers. Besides, Mindy was still greeting VIPs. Rita was ordering room service. Courtney was likely in the hotel lounge slamming Red Bull martinis. Gretchen wouldn't be teetering across this cobblestone in her spiked heels.

Tourists were snapping pictures, vendors were selling souvenir trinkets, and a street performer was playing...wineglasses? Several dozen wineglasses in various styles, filled with different water levels, lined a table. An older man lightly swept his fingers across the glass rims as if playing the classical tune on a harp or a piano.

I watched him in awe, mesmerized. "How cool..."

Declan shrugged. "Big deal. I can play 'Danny Boy' bouncing cents into shot glasses of whiskey."

I laughed. "Your talents never cease."

"Well, you mightn't realize it was 'Danny Boy' if I weren't singing along."

I snapped a selfie of us with the musician, then tossed a few korunas in the guy's hat sitting on the cobblestone.

"I can't believe the amount of action there is for this late," I said.

"It's only nine. Some people are just heading to dinner. But a bit odd no artists are out tonight." Declan paused by a lantern and released my hand. He slipped the worn leather backpack from his shoulders and unzipped it. He took out a sketch pad and pencils. "Thought I'd give ya a feel for the city's artistic ambiance."

I tried to hide my shock. Declan hadn't drawn since the death of his wife, Shauna, three years ago. In Paris, we'd visited the artsy Montmartre area, where Declan had admitted giving up art when he'd lost his muse. When I'd suggested that drawing my parents an anniversary gift might help his muse return, an awkward moment had occurred. His muse had been Shauna. He'd apologized for ever mentioning his wife and then grew distant for most of the trip. I'd been devastated that he'd regretted confiding in me, and it'd been a step backward in our relationship. This was a huge step forward.

Declan now wanted *me* to be his muse.

I choked down the lump of emotion in my throat. "That'd be great."

Declan positioned me near a lantern. He unwrapped

the blue mohair scarf around my neck, his knuckles grazing my breasts. Even through my red wool jacket, his touch caused a rush of heat up my neck. I slipped off my blue knit beret and smoothed a hand over my unruly hair.

"Make my hair look better than it does."

He smiled, tucking strands behind my ear, his fingers warm against my skin. "It looks grand."

Yeah, right. A breeze tousled Declan's hair, giving it a sexy windblown look.

He brushed a gentle kiss across my lips. I stared into his blue eyes. Our lips just inches apart, he exhaled, his warm breath visible in the cold air. I inhaled it, sharing the same breath that had moments before filled his lungs. He smiled, then backed up a few steps, trying to determine the best location to stand. I let out a contented sigh.

I peered across the river at a building washed in a hue of red for tomorrow's holiday. The restaurant we were supposed to dine at. Dinner would never have been as romantic as Declan sketching my portrait. Not that he couldn't have done it after dinner, but I was trying to remain positive.

How was I going to beat Taytos and this?

"Don't be needing to stand stiff as a board." Declan propped the sketchpad against a hip and poised the pencil over it. "Just relax, talk."

I rested back against the stone bridge, swiping hair from my face, focusing on the soft sound of fingers dancing across wineglasses. My phone dinged in my purse. I tensed. Now what? I needed to trap a *mouse* in Mr. Gauthier's room?

"Better check your mobile," Declan said.

I reluctantly whipped my phone out of my purse. It was an e-mail, rather than a text, from George Wood.

Dear Ms. Shaw,

I was most thrilled to learn you are currently in Prague, as I find myself in Vienna this week. Since you are merely a short train ride away, might I suggest I travel to Prague for a visit? Any evening would be more than suitable for me. Preferably somewhere private to allow us a proper visit. My mother was Isabella Daly. I look forward to meeting you and discussing the history of Bridget and John Michael Daly.

Kind regards,
George Wood

My shoulders sagged with disappointment that George was related to the Dalys and not Grandma. I'd feel awful if he came here and I was too busy to meet. And it would be nice for him to also meet Rachel, who was joining me in Dublin after the St. Paddy's Day meeting. We were going to visit our newfound Coffey rellies, as Rachel had canceled the visit at Christmastime to help Mom care for Dad after his accident. I'd suggest to George that he pop over to Ireland for a visit, assuming he lived in England. He sounded like Nigel, a proper Englishman, and Grandma and John Michael had moved to England.

I told Declan about George reaching out to me on the forum and taking the train over from Vienna to meet.

Declan wore a wary expression. "Ah, that's brilliant he supposedly has some family history about your granny, but what do you know about the bloke?"

"He's related to John Michael Daly."

"Where does he live?"

I shrugged. "Not sure. He sounds English."

"*Sounds* English? And he wants to meet in a private spot, for a proper visit?"

I nodded.

"What if he's an online stalker?"

"Preying on women desperately researching their ancestry?"

"Precisely."

"He knew that my grandma married John Michael Daly. I didn't know that when I posted on the forum. I'm sure he's fine. He sounds like a very proper Englishman. Like I could take him down if I had to."

Declan looked unconvinced. "At least have more info on him before you meet. And meet at a busy location near the hotel."

"Stop bursting my genealogy bubble."

Declan's eyes dimmed. "I'm serious."

"I know, and I love you for it." His concern was totally sweet, rather than overbearing and controlling like my ex-boyfriend Andy had been. "But I'm sure I'll be fine. Hopefully, he knows where my grandma and her husband lived. I want to walk the same streets and take in the same views as she did. Like in Killybog."

"And visit the church where their forbidden marriage took place."

"Exactly."

Declan had always shown a genuine interest in my family history. He wasn't just humoring me, as some guys would.

He stared into my eyes for several moments before glancing down and taking the plunge, starting to sketch. He raised his gaze. "Don't know why I be needing to even look at your eyes. I could draw them from memory."

If I could draw more than a stick figure, I'd also be able to sketch Declan's blue eyes from memory. Every thick, dark lash. The mischievous glint. I fell asleep nights picturing myself lying next to Declan, staring into his dreamy eyes, which I'd finally be able to do tonight.

"Looking forward to your first St. Paddy's Day in Ireland, are ya?" he asked.

I nodded. "Too bad we couldn't spend it in Killybog."

"Yeah, it's not as mad as Dublin. Carter's pub has a brilliant float. Des dresses as St. Patrick and drives his John Deere with his son Darragh dressed in a kilt. Mags step dances behind the tractor in a brightly colored outfit and curly red wig. Zoe wanted to walk one of Carrig's green sheep in the parade. He went mad. Wanker didn't find it funny a' tall."

"Did he ever figure out who dyed them?"

Declan shook his head. "My money's on Ronan Dunne."

Some prankster had dyed Declan's neighbor's sheep red and green for Christmas. Declan's sister and my new friend, Zoe, and I had herded them out of the road and back into the field. I couldn't tell you one thing going on with my parents' neighbors, yet after only a week in Ireland, I'd known all the local gossip and had felt like part of the community.

Declan continued sketching, his pencil flowing more freely and quickly. He was getting back into the groove. I would remember the Charles Bridge in Prague as the romantic spot where Declan and I took a critical step forward in our relationship. Just like I'd remember Dublin was the first place we'd met. The Musée d'Orsay in Paris, our first kiss. Grandma's childhood home in Killybog, the first time we'd said "I love you."

I couldn't wait for all the other firsts we would experience together and wondered in what exotic location they'd occur...

CHAPTER SIX

A feather-like sensation tickled my cheek, causing it to twitch. I let out a soft moan. I slowly opened my eyes, peering into Declan's blue eyes, his head resting on the fluffy pillow next to me. Silhouetted by a faint light from the bathroom, he traced a finger gently across my cheek. A smile curled the corners of his mouth. I still had on last night's clothes, whereas Declan wore a clean white shirt and jeans. His rain-scented shampoo filled the air. He'd already showered.

"I hate waking you so early," he said, his breath minty fresh. "You were wrecked. Out when ya hit the bed."

"Did I snore?"

"Like my uncle Jimmy at closing time."

I cringed at the thought. After dinner and a few glasses of wine at a café, we'd returned to the hotel and polished off the champagne. Rather than calming my nerves and stomach over sleeping with Declan, the alcohol had made me even more tired. It was romantic that Declan had apparently carried me from the couch to the bed but would have been even more romantic if I'd been awake.

"No worries. Even snoring, you looked hot. So hot I want to say feck my flight."

"I look far from hot right now." With mascara-smeared eyes and bed head.

I snagged mints from my purse on the floor and popped them into my mouth. I kissed Declan, sharing a mint with him. Lips locked, he eased me back on the bed. After a heated kiss that left me mint-less, he propped an elbow next to me and rested his chin on his hand, peering into my eyes.

"You should have woken me up earlier," I said. "I'm sorry I fell asleep."

"We both needed sleep." He glanced at the clock on the nightstand—5:00 a.m. "Besides, I want to make love when we can sleep in and I'm not running to catch a plane and you might have to catch a cricket."

True. Having sex for the first time carried enough pressure without the crazy work stress. And it felt reassuring that Declan no longer had a love 'em and leave 'em attitude.

He traced a finger down my cheek, causing my breath to catch in my throat.

"I need to go. Couldn't get a nonstop, so I have a connector in Frankfurt."

Flights never canceled when you wanted them to.

I reluctantly dragged myself out of bed.

I removed a pink envelope from the desk drawer and handed it to Declan. "Happy Valentine's Day. But open it later."

Declan let out a frustrated groan. "Shite. I never remember cards."

"Good. At least I got you something you didn't get me."

He wrapped me in his arms and kissed me senseless. Like he wouldn't be kissing me again for four weeks...

Stay strong!

He rested his forehead against mine, staring deep into my eyes. "Love you."

I swallowed the lump of emotion in my throat. "Love you too."

He stepped backward down the hallway, blowing me kisses, which I caught and placed against my lips. He smiled. I managed a feeble smile until he disappeared inside the elevator. I wanted to run after him. To jet off to Florence so we could spend our days visiting museums and eating gelato and our evenings making love...

I had to determine what lingering Andy issue was causing my stomach problems. I'd go straight to see Martha when I returned home. Reaching out to the women's counselor was a sign of strength, not weakness, as I'd once thought. Andy had taken a lot from me.

No way was he taking Declan.

I shut the door and collapsed against it, tears warming my cheeks. I peered over at Declan's sketch of me propped up against the lamp. He'd captured the smile in my eyes as well as on my lips. And my hair looked way better than I was sure it had. Wisps appeared to be blowing delicately against my cheeks, not whipping my face. Lights from Prague Castle twinkled behind me. I was going to hang it on my bedroom wall next to Declan's painting, which his mom had given me at Christmas.

I wiped away my tears and inhaled a calming breath. I couldn't allow myself to fall into a funk, devouring cans of chocolate frosting and not showering for days. Luckily, I was in Prague working, so I had a reason to get out of bed, or I'd be crawling back into it.

Besides needing a purpose in life, and money, seeing Declan was one of the main reasons I'd stuck with this job when I despised flying and was looking for a full-time one in Milwaukee. Meeting up with Declan in exotic locales had sounded romantic but was proving more difficult than I'd imagined. If we didn't work the same meetings, when were we going to see each other? Call me needy, but one night in six weeks wasn't enough.

We had to work more meetings together.

I'd submitted résumés to his clients, but I needed to touch base and let them know I had availability, without sounding desperate. Specifically, the dates and destinations Declan was working. I also had to make the most of our time together and not have a meltdown over capturing a stupid cricket. So much of this job was out of my control. However, I had control over how I reacted to situations. Giving Mr. Gauthier my key undoubtedly wouldn't be my last mishap. When I got frazzled, I made stupid mistakes. I'd only seen Rachel melt down under pressure once, which had led to us reconnecting after we'd grown apart, thanks to my ex and Rachel's demanding job. Yet keeping stress bottled up inside was causing her kidney problems.

I needed to actually *be* calm, not just *look* it.

I had to learn to balance my professional and personal lives. Besides needing to spend more time with Declan, I couldn't let my entire personal routine go to hell every time I traveled for work. I'd never had to sacrifice one for the other before. In college, I'd worked a no-brainer job as an elf during my Christmas breaks. My first "real" job was an admin assistant. It hadn't put a lot of demands on my time, which was good because Andy's demands were all I could handle. The biggest stress at that job was when he'd stalked me, making me a basket case and getting me fired.

Declan was the only planner I knew who handled the job in stride. Working this meeting with experienced staff would provide me with the perfect opportunity to learn how to manage the job and personal life from pros. No matter what obstacles were thrown at me today, I was going to remain Zen. Nobody was going to die if I gave a VIP my room key by mistake. Maybe I wouldn't even get fired over it.

I didn't want to lose my job, sanity, and especially not Declan.

A text alert shrilled. Declan.

Gretchen was out running and saw me get into a taxi.

As if that skinny bitch needed to run more!

Now, she was really going to make my life a living hell!

Deep breath. Stay Zen...

And stay away from Gretchen as much as possible today.

CHAPTER SEVEN

I did yoga breathing as I walked into the office a half hour before my start time, enabling me to ease into the day and not have to hit the ground running. Courtney was at the back table, facing the wall and her computer. She and Rita were cross-checking a report against a stack of printed name badges. Courtney ripped up a badge, her hand hitting a can of Red Bull, sending it flying across the room.

Blair rolled her dark eyes, then focused back on her computer.

Courtney looked ready to go off the deep end.

I raced over and reached down for the can, flinching at the shooting pain in my bruised shoulder. I snatched up the can. "I'll wipe it up." Luckily, the gold splatters matched the carpet color.

Courtney's expression relaxed slightly. "Thanks."

Our first conversation.

She returned to her task, and I used a gold linen napkin to soak up the spill.

I sat next to Gretchen, who was slashing red lines through the typed remarks on the revised event orders. My body tensed, causing my shoulder to throb. I massaged it. The office was not conducive to my Zen plan for today.

What if Gretchen confronted me about Declan? Or told Blair that I'd breached my contract by having him as an overnight guest? No, if she got me kicked off the program, she'd lose her support. As if I'd been much support.

I needed to make myself indispensable so Gretchen wouldn't want me fired from the meeting.

Good luck with that.

I set my computer bag on the desk, acting like nothing had happened. Gretchen's brow furrowed, her top lip twisted into a faint sneer. She looked the same as usual.

Maybe she'd gotten over Declan. Maybe she and Chad were now an item and she'd moved on. Maybe my debt had disappeared overnight and the government had forgiven my student loans...

Rather than flashing Gretchen a victorious grin, as she would undoubtedly do to me, I gave her a pleasant good morning.

She managed a strained smile. "Good morning."

A name badge sat on my desk. A plastic holder contained a paper badge with my name in black typeface and was clipped to a pink lanyard. This was my first meeting requiring a badge.

A text chimed on my phone. I opened it and smiled at a photo of Zoe, my dog Mr. MacCool, and her cat Quigley in matching red knitted sweaters with a candy heart across the front of each. Zoe's read *Love*. Mr. MacCool's read *Pet Me*. Quigley's read *Bite Me*. Zoe, her grandma, and her aunt had a cottage industry, selling knitted animal apparel.

I'd won Mr. MacCool in Dublin at Christmas thanks to Bernice and Gracie entering me in a contest. Unable to easily bring a dog back to the States, Zoe had offered to adopt him. Yet I still thought of him as *my* dog. I'd named him after Finn MacCool, the kick-ass hunter-warrior in Irish mythology. Legend had it he'd built the Giant's Causeway as stepping-stones to Scotland to battle a rival giant. And he'd once scooped up part of Ireland to fling it at an enemy, but it landed in the Irish Sea and became known as the Isle of Man.

I missed Zoe, Ireland, a dog I'd never met, and even antisocial Quigley. If I started losing my Zen today, I'd imagine myself in a matching sweater, curled up on the couch with Mr. MacCool in Zoe's parents' living room. The earthy scent of peat from their green cast-iron stove filled my head along with thoughts of Zoe and me chatting about Declan sketching my portrait.

I thanked Zoe and attached a pic I'd taken of the sketch.

The difficult part about being friends with Declan's sister was deciding what to share. I didn't want him to think I was always blabbing stuff to Zoe. Yet whenever possible, I tried to give Zoe and her mom hope that Declan was on the emotional road to recovery from Shauna's death.

Moments later a text popped up filled with smiley faces, hearts, and sheep. I let out a faint laugh.

Gretchen shot me an annoyed look.

Not wanting to alienate her any more than I already had today, I headed toward the breakfast room on the other side of the air wall. Blair was typing away and didn't even acknowledge me as I escaped past her desk. Mindy and Chad were just sitting down to breakfast. I gave them a wave and went through the buffet. Part of balancing my lifestyle was making healthier eating choices. No desserts, comfort foods, or wine. Well, maybe *less* wine, since I needed something to look forward to after this day. It was easy to overeat when all the food was prepared by a chef and I hated cooking. I took a scoop of eggs for protein but skipped the sausage and greasy bacon. I spooned yogurt into a bowl and added fresh berries. I put two teabags in a cup of hot water, allowing myself one cup of caffeine. I couldn't get too crazy.

I joined Chad and Mindy at a table draped in a red linen with a red rose in a glass vase in honor of the romantic holiday. Chad's pink-and-red striped tie was flipped up across his shoulder to avoid food stains. Mindy had on a pair of pink crystal earrings once again matching her lipstick. Her pink clipboard sat on the table beside her. Was she this color coordinated for every client? Her professionalism and organization reminded me of Rachel.

"Love your earrings," I said.

"Thanks. The gift shop has them in every color. They're big here. And thanks so much for taking care of Mr. Gauthier's '*challenge*.'" She made air quotes, imitating Blair. "Catching his cricket."

Chad rolled his eyes. "The guy can't catch his own cricket?"

Mindy shook her head. "It wasn't even a cricket. It was a sound machine. It's crazy there aren't two staff working VIPs."

There weren't? I'd been helping out with VIPs way more than food and beverage.

I smiled. "No problem. What'd you guys do last night?"

"I had a FaceTime dinner with my hubby," Mindy said. "That's how we've celebrated Valentine's Day the past four years. This meeting always falls on the same dates, and I didn't know what time I'd get off tonight. But it'd be worse to miss Christmas."

Chad nodded, glancing up from his cell. "I spent New Year's Eve flying over the Atlantic this year, the Pacific last year."

What a depressing time to be alone. I'd had to fly home alone from Ireland at Christmas, but at least I'd spent the morning with Declan and that night with my family.

"How many days a year are you guys gone?" I asked.

"A hundred and forty-eight last year," Mindy said. "But I just dropped a client. Found out some new guy was taking groups to Tuscany while I was in Dallas cleaning hair from shower drains in suites. I worked three back-to-back meetings for that ungrateful witch last fall. Had three suitcases packed before I left and twelve hours at home between trips."

I wouldn't have enough undies to pack for three trips.

Chad nodded in understanding. "I usually travel two hundred days a year but just lost a client with five annual meetings."

"How are you going to make your house payment?"

Mindy peered over at me. "He's got an incredible house on Laguna Beach. Yet he's rarely home."

"It'll be my retirement home. Although, I'll never retire if any more clients do. You spend years building relationships, and then a new planner comes in with her own team."

I couldn't decide if it made me feel better or worse that even experienced contractors had to find new clients and didn't know what the next year would bring. I certainly couldn't ask either of these guys to recommend clients. They wouldn't take the chance of losing work right now. I'd reached out to Declan's clients again before coming down. Fingers crossed. I should ask Rachel for some contacts. She seemed to have more faith in my abilities now, having me work at her office last month to help with Flanagan's February meeting. Yet she hadn't offered to give me referrals.

"At least Blair just contracted us for that Monte Carlo incentive." Mindy was spreading peanut butter on an English muffin, so she didn't notice the fleeting look of surprise on Chad's face.

"Ah, I was already booked so won't be doing it," he said.

Mindy glanced over at me. "She still needs staff and sounded like she's going to ask you. It'd be mid-May."

"Wonderful."

I was available, of course, and Declan would be nearby in Geneva at that time. I'd extend a few days to see him. We'd also planned to meet up in Chicago for a long weekend in April. He had a bazillion frequent flyer miles. The thought of seeing each other four months in a row made our being apart now a bit more bearable.

Rita dropped down in a chair next to me with a plateful of bacon and a Diet Coke. She rubbed her temples. "Found ten more attendees that were deleted from the database. The hotel is almost sold out. Registration is going to be a bloody nightmare. Good thing it's only two hundred people."

"*Only* two hundred?" I said.

Rita gazed at me over the top of the red glasses on the tip of her nose. "I just got off a fifteen-hundred-person sales meeting, and my next one is two waves of five hundred." She devoured several strips of bacon.

My heart raced at the thought of that many attendees.

Chimes rang out. I was going for a more Zen tone on my phone. It was a text from Gretchen. Seriously? Why hadn't she just poked her head in from next door?

Need to get product to VIP meeting.

"I gotta go." I snagged a bagel off the buffet and stashed it in my purse. So much for cutting carbs.

But I was still determined to cut my stress...

Only ten VIPs were going to be attending the sampling meeting. As if Gretchen needed my help carrying a small box containing product and the checklist. Did she plan to get me alone so she could corner me about Declan? Or lock me in a meeting room on the windowless lower level? My upper lip started to sweat as we walked in silence down a narrow hallway with red-and-gold patterned carpeting. I wanted to confront her about having seen Declan, but I wasn't sure if that would ease the tension or make it worse. And every time I blurted out something, it seemed to be a mistake.

However, when I'd blurted out Shauna's name at Christmas, it had forced Declan to eventually confront his feelings, even though it had been totally awkward at the time.

The small boardroom contained a massive wooden table surrounded with gold leather executive chairs rather than the standard black ones. I set an individual silver-packaged product marked *NOC List*—its *Mission Impossible* codename—by each china plate while Gretchen checked it off. Not knowing what was inside the plain wrapper made me want to rip it open and sneak a peek.

Gretchen had me stash two extra products under a skirted table.

"Wait here until Ted with security comes," she said.

"When will that be?"

She gave me an exasperated look. "When he gets here."

Was she sticking me in the dungeon because of Declan?

"Sounds good," I chirped, needing to be perky and supportive, even if it killed me.

"Don't forget to tell Ted the extra product is under the table or shit will hit the fan." She strutted off.

They acted like one bite of these new desserts was going to enable a person to miraculously drop ten pounds.

A half hour later, I'd counted seventy-eight red swirls, fifty gold swooshes, and thirty gold circles in the patterned carpet. My vertigo was kicking in.

My phone chimed. An e-mail from George Wood.

Dear Ms. Shaw,
My coming to Prague to meet is no trouble. Please confirm if the night after tomorrow might suit you.
Kind regards,
George Wood

Apparently, he wasn't interested in meeting up in Ireland next month. I decided to Google the man, still going on the assumption that he lived in England. It turned out there were over two hundred George Woods in the UK. I'd tell him to meet me in the busy bar next to the hotel.

I was preparing to count the white ceiling tiles when Ted, the security guy, arrived. He was mid-forties, wearing a dark suit and a serious look. He reminded me of a guard at Buckingham Palace, where you wanted to wave a hand in front of his face to try and make him blink or crack a smile. He had on a Bluetooth earbud. He was taking this whole *Mission Impossible* thing very seriously. I advised him of the stashed product.

His gaze narrowed on the front of my jacket. "Where's your name badge?"

"Oh, it's on my desk."

"You need to wear it at all times."

"Yeah, sorry about that. I'm not used to wearing one."

He arched a curious brow.

Never having worn a name badge flagged me as a newbie. Not something I wanted known.

"I usually wear a magnetic one engraved with my name." Like the hotel staff. I couldn't believe I'd just lied to security. It was more of a fib.

"And my team needs to be notified if an attendee loses a badge so we can keep an eye out for the name and make sure nobody unauthorized tries to use it to gain access to a room."

I nodded. "Will do."

I headed back to the office and slipped my badge lanyard around my neck. Before Gretchen could assign my next task, Blair marched over to me, her lips pressed firmly together. "I need Caity to run out and pick up a few things. Mr. Gauthier needs a good bottle of absinthe and white handkerchiefs. And Andrea Callan's mental health box is hung up in customs."

Gretchen rolled her eyes. "Big surprise. She probably shipped some forbidden food again."

My heart raced. Had Mr. Gauthier told Blair *why* he needed hankies? Hopefully, he didn't expect them to be monogrammed with blue embroidery.

Blair handed me a shopping list and 10,000 korunas from petty cash. The idea of walking around Prague with around $500 in cash freaked me out, but not as much as the long list: lavender air freshener, lavender soap, chamomile tea...

Finding this woman a therapist in Prague would be a much simpler task.

"I'll also have you do her souvenir shopping so that's done."

I couldn't imagine farming out my souvenir shopping

to someone. Effort and thought should go into selecting the perfect gift for loved ones. Like the Coffey pins I'd bought for Rachel and Mom in Dublin. My pin was attached to my purse strap.

"It just says *stack dolls* for her eight-year-old daughter," I said. "No color preference or suggestions. What if she doesn't like my choice and the stores won't allow me to exchange it?"

"Don't worry," Blair said. "She's not that picky. She once had us wrap the gifts without even looking at them. And make sure you negotiate a great price. She always wants to know she got a deal even though she makes a ton."

"I don't think shops deal here," Gretchen said. "At least I've never had any luck. Maybe street vendors do."

"I'm sure Caity is up to the *challenge*," Blair said.

The word *challenge* was beginning to get on my nerves.

"Ask the concierge," Blair said. "He can also tell you where to find everything. He already confirmed their spa doesn't carry lavender-scented products."

I wasn't real keen on the spa's eucalyptus-scented toiletries in my guest room bathroom. The smell was overpowering.

I was happy to get away from the office for a few hours.

One whiff of freedom and I might not return.

Precisely why Blair had us working sixteen-hour days.

"Do shops bargain here?" I asked Tobias, the concierge, who stood behind the white marble countertop desk in the lobby.

He gave his shoulder a faint shrug. "Souvenir shops might give you a deal, depending on the items."

That didn't really answer my question.

His gaze narrowed on my extensive shopping list. "Lavender and absinthe?"

"They aren't for me."

He quirked a curious brow. "For your *friend* on the honeymoon this *summer*?"

Kind of a *cheeky* thing, wasn't he?

A dog's bark echoed across the lobby, startling me. I turned to find the elderly woman from the elevator and her little dog. With pursed lips and angry gray eyes, she scooped up her pet. The concierge smiled and said hello to Madam Petrov and her dog, Fritzie. She gave him an abrupt nod. The dog growled at me and let out another bark. The woman shot me a nasty look as she marched toward the elevator, her proper square-heeled shoes clicking against the mosaic-tiled floor.

I cringed. "She reminds me of my fourth-grade teacher, Mrs. Burkhardt."

"Madam Petrov has been staying here for over fifty years, Fritzie for more than ten. I have never seen anyone provoke such a reaction from either of them."

I gave the man an offended look. "As if it's *my* fault your hotel's elevator door is defective."

He gave me a mental eye roll, like I should have known better than to step inside a closing elevator.

Whatever.

He wrote down several stores that should sell most of the items and gave me a map with directions to a row of souvenir shops near the Charles Bridge. He gazed expectantly at me.

I'd already tipped him a thousand korunas—fifty bucks—this trip. Could I tell him that had been a retainer fee? Maybe my fee had gone toward rescuing me from the elevator. I slipped 200 korunas from my pocket and placed it on the counter.

CHAPTER
EIGHT

Restaurants, Bohemian crystal shops, and souvenir stores lined the narrow cobblestone street in Old Town, leading to the Charles Bridge. The buildings blocked the morning sun, shading the street. Tourists were just starting to wander out from their hotels. I snapped a pic of a cream-colored building with decorative green stone molding, a yellow statue of a woman seated on a balcony railing. I stared at it in awe, then snapped a pic of a pastel-blue building with white scroll designs framing the windows. I was going to run out of memory on my phone, and shopping time. I needed to focus.

However, I was overwhelmed by hundreds of painted wooden stack dolls in various shapes and sizes peering out at me through the glass windows of every shop. The fact that this VIP hadn't given me a clue as to what style she wanted for her daughter made shopping even more daunting.

Five green-and-gold painted dolls with numbers across their chests stood lined up according to height in a window. The Packers football players were one of several NFL teams. Shops obviously catered to American tourists. Dad could display them on his desk at work and store paperclips and spare change or line them up on the bar in our family room. I couldn't believe I was in Prague looking at a Packers souvenir. However, I felt bad I hadn't ever brought Dad a gift from Ireland. Next to the set sat team players in gold-logoed blue jerseys. Declan's favorite rugby team. It'd make a nice gift, but not as thoughtful as Taytos and my sketch.

I stepped inside the shop, and two sales ladies gave me an obligatory nod, continuing to chat, ignoring me and the couple browsing. Besides stack dolls, the place sold souvenir mugs, magnets, plates, and other trinkets. I made a beeline for the Prince William and Catherine, Duchess of Cambridge, dolls. Zoe and I loved William and Kate. Yet my gaze strayed to a set of Santa Claus and his reindeer. I couldn't afford to buy everyone dolls. Yet if the shops didn't negotiate, maybe they'd cut me a deal if I purchased more sets. Rachel had brought me back a set of traditional stack dolls from Russia. They sat on my bedroom dresser. I needed to focus on the VIP's dolls, even though this would likely be my only chance to venture out during shop hours. I should be allowed a half hour of guilt-free souvenir shopping. Nobody ever worried about infringing on my personal time.

It would be part of my new life-balancing plan.

I spied a colorful set of Disney Princess dolls. Perfect. Unless the little girl was a tomboy.

I didn't have time to go into each shop looking for

the best price. I stepped outside and called Rachel to make sure Gretchen hadn't been lying, just to make my life more difficult, about vendors not negotiating. And the concierge had been a bit vague. I also wanted to tell her about Declan sketching me on the bridge, since she knew he'd given up art. We'd attempted to hide our relationship from my sister on our Dublin meeting at Christmas, worried she'd question Declan's playboy reputation and our ability to remain professional. When she'd discovered we were seeing each other, she hadn't approved, afraid that I'd end up getting hurt again. One lousy boyfriend choice and nobody trusted my judgment in men.

I explained my shopping task to Rachel.

"Gretchen says they don't negotiate here."

"Yeah, I've never had much luck there. Yet I've only bought some small perfume bottles. It's off-season, though. They might come down. Start walking away and see if they follow you."

That didn't sound promising.

I told her about George Wood contacting me and coming over from Vienna for a visit.

"Did you bring your pepper spray?" she asked.

I rolled my eyes. "You sound like Declan." And Mom, who'd obviously told Rachel I traveled with defense spray. Usually.

"Well, I agree this guy sounds a bit suspicious, traveling hours to meet up with you to discuss family history."

"I'm meeting him at a busy bar next to the hotel." I couldn't allow Declan and her to make me paranoid, or I'd end up canceling with George.

"That's good. Hopefully, he's legit."

I veered the conversation away from a possible online stalker to Declan's sketch.

"Wow, that's a big step for him. I'm happy for you. Really. One less thing to worry about."

How many things did she still think I had to worry about with Declan? I'd confided in her about my relationship with Andy, but I was hesitant to discuss the physical issue possibly preventing me from sleeping with Declan. She'd tell me it was a sign that I shouldn't sleep with him, but it felt right. Once I got my stomach problems solved.

"I got a card from Gerry." Her tone was matter of fact.

"How romantic is that? He mailed a handwritten card from Ireland when he could have just texted or sent an e-card."

"Yeah, that was nice of him."

Nice of him? As if this guy was a hotel sales rep or a casual acquaintance. They'd had sex in every room of his townhouse. He owned Coffey's pub in Dublin. On my first meeting, Rachel had taken the staff to dinner at our surname pub hoping there'd be a family connection. There wasn't unless it went back several generations. Rachel always downplayed her feelings, but I sensed she really liked Gerry. But did he realize she did?

"Did you call him?" I asked.

"No, I e-mailed and told him I got it. I'm sure the pub was crazy busy with Valentine's Day."

Today was Valentine's Day, and the pub likely hadn't even opened yet. I loved that Rachel and I could now talk boys, and I felt she needed some sisterly advice.

"You should call him."

My phone chimed in my ear, startling me.

"Hold one sec."

I should have changed my text alert for Gretchen to a tornado siren.

What's your status?

I just started shopping.

It would take me hours to fulfill the woman's insane shopping list. I refused to let other people's stress become my stress. However, the later I returned, the later I'd be working tonight.

Deep breath...

My text sounded a bit snippy. Since I'd decided I needed to suck up, I added: *Will hurry back as soon as possible.*

I told Rachel I had to run.

A guy stood outside the shop next door, smoking a cigarette, pitching his business to passersby. He appeared more eager to make a sale and possibly negotiate than the chatty women in the other shop. As I approached, he flicked his cigarette into the street.

"Come. I give you very good price, Caity."

"How'd you know my name?"

He gestured to the badge hanging around my neck.

As he ushered me inside, I buttoned up my coat. Walking around Prague displaying a name badge was probably safe unless some weirdo followed me back to the hotel. Wearing one at the hotel wasn't real secure. If someone followed me off the elevator and learned my room number, they could charge up a storm to my account. Not to mention stalk me.

The same dolls as the other shop filled the shelves.

A nervous feeling fluttered in my stomach. I gestured to the Disney Princess dolls. "How much are those?"

"For you, two thousand korunas."

"What if I also buy those?" I pointed at the smaller set of Packer dolls.

"One thousand five hundred each."

"They're half the size."

I should have asked Declan for negotiating tips. With his Irish charm, he could talk anyone into giving him something for nothing. Had he landed in Florence yet?

"I'll be right back," I said. "I need to call my boyfriend."

"Wait," he yelled after me as I headed toward the door. "How much so you don't need to call boyfriend?"

A worried expression furrowed the man's brow. Was he concerned that if I called my boyfriend, he'd tell me not to buy the dolls?

"Fifteen hundred for the big set, nine hundred for the smaller one," I said.

"One thousand one hundred for small one."

"One thousand. And I'll also take the William and Kate dolls and the Santa ones."

He nodded in defeat.

I smiled triumphantly, anxious to brag to Gretchen about my bargaining skills.

He gave me directions to the first store the hotel's concierge had recommended for mental health items and absinthe.

Just up the street, a guy standing in a shop's doorway held out two watercolor prints of the Charles

Bridge from different views. They were done in gorgeous autumn-colored hues bordered in a burgundy matte. My mind filled with memories of Declan sketching me on the romantic bridge. They'd make the perfect gift for him. He'd one day have an apartment to hang them in.

"You like?" the man asked.

"How much?"

"Seven hundred fifty korunas. Er, thirty-five dollars."

Wait a sec. I'd just paid a thousand korunas for a small set of stack dolls, thinking I was paying twenty-five bucks, not fifty. Was this guy's calculation right? I typed it into the currency conversion app on my phone. Crap. I'd been so excited and caught up in negotiating, I hadn't been thinking clearly. Ugh. Could I expense seventy-five bucks for the VIP's dolls? Would Blair think that still sounded like a deal?

A man hollered down the street in Czech.

Our gazes darted to a police officer running toward us.

The guy scooped up a large black plastic bag in the doorway and took off, leaving me holding the prints. The officer glanced at me as he raced past. He yelled out to the guy, who disappeared around a corner with his black bag in tow. What the hell? He was selling the prints out of a bag? I'd thought he was standing outside a shop, trying to lure people in with his beautiful artwork, like the other guy.

I'd almost bought hot prints for Declan.

Instead, I'd gotten them for *free*.

Could I get arrested for unknowingly accepting stolen merchandise? Maybe the prints weren't stolen.

The guy just didn't have a sales permit. Or maybe he was dating the police officer's sister and the man was pissed off. There could be dozens of reasons why the cop was chasing him.

Yet I escaped down the street in the opposite direction, thankful that I'd buttoned up my coat so the officer hadn't seen my name. If I had to use the rest of petty cash for bail money, Blair would send me home on the next plane.

CHAPTER NINE

I zipped through the hotel's side entrance, weighted down with bags, and made a beeline for the elevator bank. My gaze darted toward the lobby, then over my shoulder. I stabbed the elevator button, glancing around. If anyone were watching me, they'd think I'd just heisted a bank and was on the run. It wasn't that I was in a rush to stash potentially hot prints in my room. I didn't want my coworkers to discover I'd bought myself souvenirs while running VIP errands. Gretchen and Blair would think that had delayed me.

Several things had delayed me. Frazzled after the print encounter, I'd gone the wrong direction and gotten totally lost. I'd had to find an ATM for cash after overpaying for the stack dolls, which left me with only four hundred dollars in my account. And it'd taken three stores to find everything on the woman's extensive mental health list. What about *my* mental health? What happened to deserving a half hour to buy souvenirs?

My phone chimed. I tensed, then relaxed when I saw it was from Declan rather than Gretchen.

At hotel in Florence. Your card makes me miss ya even more.

Recalling the card's mushy, borderline sappy sentiments made my eyes water.

Me too. And I just picked you up some hot prints.

Luv you.

I smiled. *Love you too.*

I made it to my room without encountering anyone I knew. I tossed my bags and prints on the floor inside the door. Mission accomplished. I zipped down to the office, sneaking into the meal room to grab lunch before Blair or Gretchen put me to work. No food buffet. I'd texted Gretchen I was on my way back, which was probably why she'd pulled it. I should have grabbed a few bags of Taytos from my room. I snatched a candy bar from a basket, then reluctantly exchanged it for a banana and a small bag of mixed nuts.

Remain Zen...

I hummed "Santa Claus Is Coming to Town," trying to drown out Mindy's phone conversation demanding the status of a VIP's bag delivery, the top popping on Courtney's energy drink, fingers pounding laptop keys, and printers frantically spitting out paper. Christmas carols usually helped me relax.

Blair pounced on me before I could turn and escape. "How'd it go?"

"Great." Except I'd forked out double the korunas from what I'd originally thought. The fact that the hot prints offset the extra cost of the dolls wasn't comforting. I showed Blair the souvenirs and mental health items.

She eyed the handkerchiefs with interest. One was plain white, the other white with blue trim, resembling the one Mr. Gauthier had given to Madam Petrov. Was Blair upset both weren't white?

"Is something wrong?" I asked innocently.

She shook her head. "No. Should be fine. Andrea Callan doesn't land for a few hours, so you can prepare her room. Spray it, lay magazines on the cocktail table. Stuff like that."

Gretchen glared at Blair, then peered over at me. "I need you to shadow the minibar attendant to make sure he swaps out the competitor products with Evans and Walker ones in all the regular rooms checking in tonight. Mindy has checked the suites."

"Absolutely." I smiled. "I'll hurry and get this done so I can help out with that."

Gretchen looked surprised by my eagerness to assist when Blair seemed to care less if she had support. Besides me needing to suck up, it was ridiculous that I kept getting pulled in every direction because this meeting was understaffed. Everyone was suffering.

I headed up to Ms. Callan's suite. Luckily, the room wasn't as big as the Presidential Suite...or haunted. That I knew anyway. The room was decorated in gold, yellow, and blue. I fanned magazines on the cocktail table. Luckily, a kiosk had sold ones in English. The air freshener cans were in Czech, so I'd relied on pictures. I didn't know for sure what lavender looked like, but I'd bought a can with a purple flower on it. I sprayed the air. I took a whiff, deciding it was lavender. Mmm... I sprayed the air again and stepped through the mist so the scent would linger on my clothes. I should have bought a can for my room.

Bingo. I had to add a mental health bag to my packing list to make my guest room a Zen Zone. Balance. I now knew where to find all the needed products in Prague. I just had to find the *time* to shop for them, especially the luxurious open-toe spa slippers. My feet were killing me from walking and running miles on uneven cobblestone streets and sidewalks. I had no clue how American shoe sizes compared to European ones. I pulled the slippers from the bag and studied the size forty pair. They looked big. If I was dropping money on spa slippers, they'd better fit. I sat down on the comfy blue velvet chair to quickly try one on. I slid a stockinged foot into a slipper and curled my toes into the cushiony softness. I tried on the other slipper. I slowly relaxed back into the chair, easing out a relaxed moan...

My eyes shot open. It took a moment to realize I was in Ms. Callan's suite. Panic raced through me. Omigod. I'd dozed off! My gaze darted to the antique clock on the wall. I'd left the office forty-five minutes ago!

Noise came from the master bedroom.

Someone was in the suite.

Or, some*thing*.

Hopefully, this suite was also haunted.

I slouched down in the chair facing opposite the bedroom. If the VIP had checked in, either she hadn't seen me, or she was calling security from the other room. My breathing quickened. I had to get out of here!

I quietly stood and tiptoed toward the door, slippers slapping against my feet. My gaze darted to my shoes on the carpet by the chair. I turned around to grab them when Mindy walked out of the bedroom. We both let out a startled squeal.

"Omigod, you scared the hell out of me," Mindy said, hand to her chest.

I took a deep, calming breath. "I'm sorry."

"I tried calling you to see if the Evans and Walker amenity was delivered, but you didn't answer."

I'd been so out I hadn't heard my phone ringing? Had Gretchen texted me, wondering where I was?

"Ah, sorry. This room seems to be a dead zone."

Mindy paled, as if this room might also be haunted.

I glanced down at the slippers on my feet. "You're probably wondering why I'm wearing these." Mindy was a consummate professional. I was surprised she wasn't flippin' out on me. Would she tell Blair?

Mindy's forehead crinkled. "Yeah, kind of."

"My feet were killing from running around on cobblestone for hours. I wanted to buy a pair of these slippers but needed to know the size first." Unsure if she realized I'd been snoozing in the chair, I didn't mention it. "I'm sorry." I quickly exchanged the slippers for my shoes, my feet protesting against the firm rubber soles.

She nodded in understanding, her blue eyes dimming. "I was once on a horrible program in Edinburgh, making VIP amenity deliveries every night while the rest of the staff went out for fancy dinners. There was a four-hundred-dollar bottle of scotch in a suite from the previous night's delivery. I slammed a fifty-dollar glass."

My eyes widened with shock, unable to picture Mindy doing such a thing. It would be like Rachel doing it.

"It wasn't as if the guy had paid for it. I considered it combat pay and for having to eat room service hamburgers every night."

"I'm not judging—believe me. I'm just...surprised."

"And I had another glass in the next suite," she said matter of factly.

"Your secret is safe with me."

She gave me a conspiratorial smile as she walked out the door. "So is yours."

It felt good that Mindy had trusted me with her secret. Most of mine were mishaps I was too embarrassed to share. Had Rachel ever been so stressed out she'd slammed a VIP's two-hundred-dollar bottle of wine or spritzed herself with their expensive perfume? Or how about Gretchen? Maybe they weren't as straitlaced and professional as they appeared. And everyone slipped up once in a while.

I would kill to know Rachel's and Gretchen's secrets.

⁊❦ ❧⁊

When I returned to the office, a note from Gretchen sat on my desk, with the minibar attendant's contact number. Maybe she'd been gone and hadn't noticed my absence. The office was empty except for Rita and Courtney, who were now both slamming energy drinks and cross-checking reports.

"We might be rooming together," Courtney told Rita. "Here's another one without a room." She lowered her voice. "You'd think Blair would appreciate us cleaning up this mess. My usual planner is awesome.

No way am I working for this bitch again. I got stuck on this meeting because I was stupid enough to say yes after two others refused. I wanted to be a *team* player."

"This is a rough one, luv." Rita couldn't outright agree when Blair controlled her future job prospects.

"The only reason she keeps her job is because she's sleeping with a vice president, Mr. Gauthier. She must be a dynamo in bed. They try to never be seen together, since they're both married, which makes it even more obvious."

Mr. Gauthier and Blair?

Was that why she'd eyed the hanky with interest? She knew his old one had blue trim and she'd wondered how *I'd* known that? What if their pillow talk had included my sucky French and Mr. Gauthier's hanky being used to wipe up dog pee? If his English was so poor, how did they communicate? Maybe the fact that they *couldn't* was how he tolerated Blair.

I broke out in a sweat.

If Mr. Gauthier had said anything to Blair, she'd have taken me off VIPs. Right? Yet, who else was available to solve his cricket issue and make his absinthe run? That was likely why I kept getting pulled from food and beverage. She was more concerned about her boyfriend's needs. And since she was short staffed, incompetent staff might be better than none.

I had to avoid Mr. Gauthier.

I spent the rest of the afternoon stalking the minibar guy, making sure he replaced all the competitor products with Evans and Walker ones. It took forever since pretty much anything in a minibar could be considered a dessert.

Blair's client had just arrived and wanted to review all the products with Gretchen, who had no choice but to have me work a VIP dinner by myself. My event order might as well have been written in Czech. Trying to decipher all my notes from the pre-con was nearly impossible. The comments Gretchen had emphasized as "critical" I'd highlighted in green. The entire page was green. I blew out a calming breath. After Gretchen's snide remark asking if I'd worked any meal functions since Powerscourt in Ireland, this dinner had to go perfectly.

The banquet server—Armando from Italy—watched me open chafing dishes and check items against the menu. Salmon, chicken, potatoes...

"Where's the soup of the day?" I asked.

He gestured to a separate table with a silver soup urn and bowls. No label.

"Items need to be labeled with allergies and dietary restrictions. Please make sure you have a vegetarian meal." Mr. Gauthier was vegetarian. "Without garlic." He was allergic. I studied my notes. "And no pepper."

I recalled Declan's story about getting fired over a CEO's pineapple allergy. Despite Declan having advised the restaurant about it, some rogue bartender was making pineapple blender drinks and the fruit became airborne, resulting in an emergency room run.

Armando nodded, strolling off in search of labels

and the special meal that I should probably taste test before serving to the VIP. Armando wasn't exactly up to snuff for such a prestigious hotel.

I looked up *garlic, pepper,* and *vegetarian* on my translation app, preparing for my conversation with Mr. Gauthier. Fifteen minutes before start time, no attendees and no Armando. What if VIPs showed up and wanted to know what items contained gluten or nuts? What if Gretchen stopped by to double-check everything?

Even worse, Mr. Gauthier was walking into the room.

So much for avoiding the man. He'd definitely have a special request. Like he was also allergic to cork and required a twist-off top on the wine.

We exchanged *bonsoirs.* I confirmed his special meal request before I forgot how to pronounce pepper, *poivre.* He gave me a pleased smile. He gestured toward the soup urn, rattling off something in French. Soup of the day? Crap. I should have asked Armando.

I lifted the top from the silver urn to identify it. A whoosh of steam rose up and scalded my pinky. I dropped the cover on the urn, letting out a squeal of pain. I stuck my finger in a punch bowl of ice, the burning sensation subsiding slightly.

"Mon dieu." The man eyed my pinky, or possibly the ice bucket, with concern. It was the ice for beverages.

I snapped my hand out of the bowl. I assured him I was fine—unless, of course, he mentioned this incident to Blair.

I diverted the conversation to wine, offering him a glass from a selection of bottles displayed on a table.

He requested a red. I was proud that I'd have understood him even if he hadn't pointed to the bottle. He tasted the wine and smiled with approval. We stood smiling at each other. I was starting to sweat. Maybe I could entertain him by playing a tune on the wineglasses like the musician the night before.

Where the hell was Armando?

Another man walked in and requested the same wine. Thankfully, they started chatting in what I believed was German.

Nervous about being able to fulfill VIPs' demands, and upset that I'd burned my finger because Armando was MIA, I texted Nigel, inquiring about the server's status. Five minutes later, Oscar from Sweden arrived with the food labels and informed me the soup was vegetable. He was the nice man who'd offered me an additional table linen when I'd been freezing in the cooler.

I requested fresh ice.

He sniffed the air. "That scent is nice."

"I think it's the white wine sauce on the salmon."

His brow wrinkled. "Ah, no, the scent on you."

I'd run out of perfume before my trip, so he was referring to the lavender air freshener. I needed to sneak out and buy some so I could douse myself in the calming scent every morning.

I smiled. "Thank you."

"You're missing the badge." Oscar pointed at my empty lanyard clip.

Where was my name badge?

The last time I'd noticed it was while I was souvenir shopping. I'd come back and gone to my room, and then I'd placed all the Zen products in the VIP suite, and then... Omigod. Had it come off in the suite? I'd been authorized to access the room, yet if Ms. Callan turned my badge in, Ted the security guy would flip out. I'd get written up. I could also have lost it in one of the twenty attendees' rooms when I was shadowing the minibar attendant.

Oscar stayed until Armando finally returned with a crappy attitude, reeking of cigarettes. He'd been on a smoke break? I didn't trust this guy not to disappear again, or Gretchen not to pop in and check up on me, but my finger was throbbing. I had to make a gift shop run for burn ointment. A hot pack for my shoulder would also be nice. Thankfully, there was no new client product, so leaving the room unattended for a few minutes before dinner was served wasn't a huge deal.

Before heading to the gift shop, I popped by the office to look for my missing badge. Luckily, nobody was there, and luckily, I had a key. I dropped down on my hands and knees and searched under my desk.

"Did you lose something?" Ted asked, walking in.

I popped up, snatching a folder off the desk, slapping it to my chest, covering the empty lanyard clip.

"An earring. It's not there."

Ted eyed the pair of earrings dangling from my ears.

"I lost it yesterday. Gotta get back to the dinner. Just needed to grab this folder."

I flew out of the office, heart thumping against my chest. I peeked inside the folder to find revised event orders. Great. I'd have to return them before Gretchen realized they were missing.

I went to the gift shop and dropped an insane amount of money on first-aid cream.

At least the shamrock and *Póg Mo Thóin*—Kiss My Ass—undies I'd paid too much for in Dublin were souvenirs and empowering. I packed them every meeting.

I slathered on the cream, but my finger still hurt. I had to start traveling with first-aid items. It was hit or miss if I'd find trusted brands in a foreign country.

I walked across the lobby toward the elevators. A dog let out a ferocious bark, startling me. Fritzie and Madam Petrov had just entered the hotel. The dog let out another bark, and people peered at me with curiosity and concern.

I gave Fritzie a sympathetic look. "You know, you're not the only one traumatized by what happened."

He growled.

So much for bonding.

The woman's gaze sharpened, and she spoke a few harsh words, likely Russian, based on her last name. I didn't need to type it into my translator app to know she wasn't wishing me a good night. I waited in the lobby, not wanting to ride the elevator up with them, massaging the stress-induced throbbing in my shoulder. The barking stopped. I peeked over to see if they'd left. Mr. Gauthier stood there petting Fritzie, who was licking his hand. I wanted to yell out, *I have a dog! Animals love me!* Madam Petrov and Fritzie got in an elevator, and the VIP went outside for a smoke. I headed toward the elevator, going to my room to search for my badge.

Funny, I considered Mom a mother hen when she insisted on checking up on me, yet she was now the first person I called for advice on my burn, and I could really use a comforting voice.

"Honey," Mom said. "Raw honey if you can find it."

"I can probably get it from the banquet department."

"My mom used honey for everything. She'd put some in warm milk to help us sleep at night and used it to lower her cholesterol. Though she never put it in her tea. She thought it an odd American custom."

Rachel and I used to drink tea and hot chocolate out of our favorite cups in Grandma's teacup collection. A collection I'd learned, from my Irish rellie Sadie Collentine, had been from our great-grandma Flannery's family porcelain factory in County Wicklow, Ireland. Thanks to my aunt Teri's hoarding issue, Teri had kept Grandma's entire collection after she died, boxing it up and sticking it in the basement rather than donating it to a thrift shop. Rachel and I had gone through the collection after Christmas, each of us selecting a half dozen cups.

Mom confirmed she and Dad had gone to the Taco Cantina, their favorite Mexican restaurant, for Valentine's Day. Unlike Rachel, Mom didn't ask how my holiday had gone with Declan, because she hadn't known about it. She thought Declan and I were just friends, and I wanted to keep it that way for a bit longer. She knew just enough about my relationship with Andy to be concerned and question my ability to select my own match.

I whisked into my room and scanned the floor for my badge.

"I was talking to Rachel, and she mentioned a distant relative contacted you," Mom said.

I hadn't planned on mentioning the visit to Mom until afterward, not wanting her to freak out like everyone else seemed to be over me meeting a stranger in Prague.

"He's not related to us. He's a Daly, related to Grandma's first husband, John Michael. But he has some family history and is nice enough to hop over to Prague while he's in Vienna."

Even though she'd taken the news about Grandma's first marriage surprisingly well, Mom wasn't joining Rachel and me on our visit to Grandma's niece after St. Paddy's Day.

I checked the desktop and dresser for my badge.

"Keep me posted. Take your pepper spray and be careful."

Strange, she was much calmer about my visit with George than Rachel or Declan had been. My relationship with Mom was going better than when I'd moved in with my parents eight months ago. She wasn't constantly inquiring about the status of my debt and hadn't sent me a job application since Cheesey Eddie's three months ago. It helped that I'd been on the road and in Rachel's office planning a Flanagan's beer meeting currently going on in Dublin. An executive's assistant had gone on-site for it.

Oh, how I wished I were working that one instead.

Mom and I said good-bye while I was on my knees looking under the bed. I was about to give up and face the fact that my badge was in the VIP's suite or an attendee's room when I grabbed my coat off the back of the chair to hang it up and my badge fell to the floor. My shoulders dropped with relief. The rough edges of the plastic holder had likely stuck to the inside of my wool coat.

I snatched up the badge and clipped it to the lanyard.

I wondered if they sold superglue in the gift shop, since I couldn't allow something as simple as a name badge to make me come unglued this meeting.

CHAPTER
TEN

After the dinner, I swung by the office. Blair was the only one there. I said a quick good night and replaced Gretchen's folder with revised event orders. Hopefully, she hadn't been searching for them. Trudging into my room at ten o'clock, I wanted to collapse onto the bed, but I had to FaceTime with Declan. It would be the only personal thing I'd done all day except for spending ten minutes buying souvenirs and burn ointment—which was work related. Putting on lipstick might look like I was trying too hard, so I brushed my hair and wiped the mascara from under my eyes. I entertained the thought of slipping on my red bra, but I didn't want our first sex to be FaceTime sex and set the tone for our intimate relationship.

Declan answered the call. A tall naked guy stood behind him—a statue lit up in the middle of a fountain. Declan wore a dark wool coat and black slacks. He was still on duty.

"Where are you?" I asked.

"The Fountain of Neptune. Wish you were here."

He panned his phone across the lively square filled with couples and restaurant windows lit up in red and pink hues. I should have made the trek to Old Town Square, but my feet were killing me. Prague's square looked romantic from the pictures I'd seen in my travel guide.

"I wish I were too." I plastered on a cheery smile to mask the aching inside me to be with Declan. *Stay strong!*

"I have a surprise for ya." His phone zoned in on a street performer dressed in a black tux, holding a guitar. Great. A romantic serenade to make me a blubbering idiot.

However, rather than "La Vie en Rose," the man broke into a lively tune. "Hey where did we go...Down in the hollow..."

Declan sliced a hand in front of his neck, cutting the guy off. "Not 'Brown Eyed Girl,' mate. I said '*Galway Girl*.'"

The performer gazed off into the night, a pensive look on his face.

Declan shook his head. "No worries." He gestured to the guitar, and the man nodded, handing Declan his instrument. Declan gave the guy his phone to take over the video call. He pretended to strum the guitar, singing without accompaniment. "Well, I took a stroll...I met a little girl...'Cause her hair was *auburn*...her eyes were *blue*..."

"Galway Girl." My favorite song from the movie *P.S. I Love You.* I burst out laughing, glad I'd combed my hair and wiped the black circles from around my eyes.

Declan hopped up on the edge of the fountain, as if he were on stage, the naked statue behind him. His voice grew louder, and he totally got into his fake guitar playing. People were gathering, snapping pics, a few clapping along. My foot was tapping in rhythm to the song.

Declan jumped down from the fountain. "...ain't nothin' like a *Milwaukee* girl!"

People clapped, and several tossed change on the ground in front of him.

"Woot, woot!" I yelled. "Brilliant!"

He took a bow, then disappeared a moment while he exchanged the guitar for his phone.

"How am I ever going to beat that?" I asked.

He smiled, catching his breath. "How about 'Frosty the Snowman'?"

Declan had walked in on me singing the Christmas carol in Paris.

His smile faded. "Ah, sorry. Have to get back to the dinner."

I tried to act upbeat, not wanting to put a damper on his romantic surprise, which turned out even more romantic than he'd planned. "We had room service pizzas in the office." Except for Rita, who'd ordered a plate of bacon. If working 1,500-person meetings didn't give her a heart attack, her comfort food would.

"We're having family-style pasta. How mad is that? Being in Italy and eating pasta." Declan laughed.

He blew me a kiss, and we said ciao.

I placed my fingertips against my lips as if the touch of Declan's kiss lingered, imagining the taste on my lips...

I had to come up with something special to do for

Declan. His birthday was in April, but I didn't know the date. I texted Zoe, who immediately responded *April 19*. The week after we were planning to meet up in Chicago. Perfect. I had to start planning something like dinner at the top of the John Hancock Center or a romantic cruise on Lake Michigan. I'd done the romantic Seine cruise in Paris by myself, and Declan had done it with fifty attendees while I'd dined with six-year-old Henry at a magician's show. Maybe I could bring the romance of Paris to Lake Michigan...

While humming "Galway Girl," I made a cup of tea, opened a bag of Taytos, and settled in at my computer to search for Chicago dinner cruises. Not cheap, but the pics of a boat cruising along the Chicago skyline lit up at night were *très* romantic. I gazed longingly at a couple drinking wine on a deck, imagining Declan as Cary Grant and myself as Audrey Hepburn in the movie *Charade*, floating down the Seine...

We were definitely doing a cruise.

I checked out Ireland's news on Facebook. I followed County Westmeath's newspaper, Carter's pub, and Peter Molloy's, and several local businesses in Killybog and Declan's hometown, Glenteen. Conway's restaurant was running a ten-euro special on chicken curry. I about gagged at the thought of the goose curry I'd nearly puked on at Finn O'Brien's cooking lesson in Dublin. Other than that, it was all *good* news.

A rap sounded at the door. I tiptoed over and peered out the peephole at Ted and a huge man in a dark suit holding a clipboard and a small jar. I'd seen him lurking around the meeting space. Why was hotel security and Ted at my door? An unannounced name badge check?

Before opening the door, I eyed my badge sitting on the desk.

Hotel security handed me a jar of honey. "From Nigel in banquets."

I hadn't yet slathered on the first jar Nigel had given me.

He gestured to his clipboard. "I need to file a report on the burn. May I enter?"

An official report?

"It's really not that bad. And was my own fault. I'm not blaming the hotel." I showed him that my bright-pink finger wasn't blistered, bleeding, or charred. Even though it felt like it.

"A formality," Ted said.

I debated stepping into the hallway or letting them into my room. Not wanting my coworkers to see us and question why security was at my door, I let them in. I answered their questions, embarrassed to admit what I'd done.

"Do you need a doctor?" Ted asked.

"No," I blurted out.

No way was I going to a hospital. If I hadn't gone after nearly dislocating my shoulder, I wasn't going for something so minor. My dad's insurance didn't cover international. I'd no longer be covered under it at all when I turned twenty-six next year. It'd be years before I'd be able to afford insurance, with my student loan kicking in. And I was starting to think I might need *disability* insurance even more than health insurance.

After they left, I stuck my finger in the jar of honey, then wrapped it in a Band-Aid so I didn't get my laptop keys sticky.

What if I'd had to go to the hospital? Major medical expenses without international insurance coverage would put me into an even deeper debt. I had to carry international health insurance even if it was just basic coverage. And in a year, I'd be responsible for full coverage. I needed to create a budget to figure out how to pull a monthly insurance premium out of my butt. I'd never kept a budget. Balancing my checkbook about sent me over the edge.

I had two meetings booked: Rachel's St. Paddy's Day meeting and Heather's May one. I hadn't received a cancellation fee for Heather's February Venice meeting, so she'd booked me on a New York one in May. I also had my Brecker bonus, the amount to still be determined. That would pay my taxes and get me through the next two months.

A half hour later, I sat slumped in the chair, staring at my budget on the computer. Alone in a hotel room on Valentine's Day was not the time to see in writing how pathetic my finances were. At the rate I was going, I'd be out of debt just in time to retire. I had to get more work. I needed to travel 150 to 200 days a year to make a serious dent in my debt. That would mean buying two more suitcases and an extra stash of undies so I could work back-to-back trips like Mindy and Declan.

I was jet-lagged just thinking about it.

Yet, how many *years* would it take me to have enough clients to *book* me two hundred days a year?

I wanted financial independence. To be able to stand on my own. I'd overextended myself trying to keep up with Andy's lifestyle and live up to his standards. And now I was paying the price.

Bernice and Gracie were still entering me in contests. Besides winning a dog, I'd won a muffin-of-the-month club subscription, which I'd given to my aunt Dottie for her birthday, and a hundred-dollar gift certificate for some barbecue restaurant chain in Texas. No big-screen TVs or lawn mowers that would bring me big bucks on Craigslist. The ladies were going to pay me the rest of my fee once I'd completed their research. They'd paid for my Ancestry.com subscription, and I was charging them a $200 flat fee for the project, rather than an hourly rate, since I spent hours trying to figure out where to even look for information. After weeks of research, I'd discovered the "sounds like" option on sites was critical for finding information that was incorrectly documented or transcribed. My $200 research fee came out to like twenty cents an hour. My event planning job paid a hundred bucks more than that *daily.*

Maybe if I won enough muffin-of-the-month clubs I could open a bakery.

∂❦ ❦∂

I woke up with my head resting against the wooden desk, a sweet taste in my mouth. I licked the sticky substance from my lips. Honey. I lifted my head, a clump of hair peeling from a gooey puddle on the desk. Ugh. I hadn't planned on washing my hair today.

I'd removed the Band-Aid and stuck my finger in the jar, which had tipped over in my sleep. A puddle had spread across the desk, coming dangerously close to my laptop. Better it was on me than my laptop. I licked the honey from my finger. The red mark had faded to a light pink, and the sting was gone. I tossed the jar in the garbage and cleaned up the sticky mess. I pulled my hair back in a clip until I could wash it.

It was 4:00 a.m. Good thing I'd woken up, since I hadn't set an alarm. Rather than entering muffin contests, I'd dozed off while researching Bernice and Gracie's family history. After a hundred research hours, I'd finally had my first breakthrough. I'd discovered the baptismal certificate for their grandpa James McKinney in Montreal, Canada, rather than Ontario, where the women thought he'd been born. My French sucked and the writing was barely legible, but I was able to translate enough to determine that his father, James Senior, was a sergeant in Her Majesty's 23rd Regiment Fusiliers. Unable to locate his military records, I'd sent an e-mail to my Irish friend Nicholas Turney—an elderly neighbor of Declan's parents—asking if he had a contact who might be able to assist with accessing the records at an archive. A local historian, Nicholas had helped me with my Coffey family research, reassuring me that my ancestor hadn't been involved in a murder.

I'd immediately e-mailed Bernice and Gracie my discovery, even though I wasn't certain if the man's military documents even existed. However, every clue was a cause for celebration and gave them, and me, more confidence in my genealogist skills.

I needed all the confidence I could get in any area of my life right now.

CHAPTER
ELEVEN

My first day of creating balance in my life hadn't been a huge success. It'd been more of a balancing *act*, and I was determined not to fall off the high wire I was teetering on. Yet I was starting off the day with little sleep, having stayed up to conduct more ancestry research. And I felt like a sticky mess even though I'd shampooed my hair four times and soaped myself down a half dozen.

Only 6:00 a.m. and the office was already bustling. Courtney and Rita were stuffing name badges into holders. I checked to make sure my badge was hanging around my neck. A stash of Red Bull was iced down in a bucket on the floor by Courtney's desk. She'd need every drop of it. Attendees arrived today.

Blair was on the phone, and Mindy and Chad were engrossed in their laptops. Gretchen had stepped out. I was scanning e-mails, including one from Declan's client offering me a Miami gig in April. Reaching out to his clients yesterday had paid off. I pulled up our

Google calendars and reconfirmed that Declan was in London that week. His clients probably hired me because he was always busy.

When had he added an Amsterdam meeting in April?

Actually, he hadn't *added* the Amsterdam meeting. His airline flight had linked to the calendar. We'd planned to meet up in Chicago that week since we wouldn't have seen each other since St. Paddy's Day. What about the romantic cruise I'd planned? My heart sank. I couldn't believe he hadn't told me about the trip.

Declan only had four open days in April. Why did he need money that badly that he had to travel nonstop? He didn't have an apartment. He crashed with his brother in London or at his parents' if he needed a place to stay. His tiny car had to be paid off. He expensed most of his food to clients. Since Shauna's death, he'd worked to escape his personal life, but he didn't still need to escape.

Did he?

I wanted to shoot him an e-mail about the Amsterdam meeting, but I feared the conversation would turn into an argument even though I was more hurt than upset that he hadn't discussed it with me. I needed to find the right moment to bring it up.

An e-mail from Nicholas Turney popped into my inbox. He provided the link to James McKinney's military records on Ancestry.com. I'd failed to locate the record because the last name was misspelled Makimey. That wasn't even close. Blair was still on the phone, so I clicked the link. A faint document appeared. Heart racing, I enlarged it for better viewing, fingers crossed. The fancy cursive penmanship with tall, skinny, loopy letters was nearly impossible to read. It should have been mandatory to print legibly on all official documents.

"Are you doing okay?" Blair materialized in front of my desk, startling me.

I closed the research site. "Ah, yeah, breakfast is set, and—"

"I mean your burn." Her tone was more annoyed than concerned.

"How did you know about my burn?"

"Ted called me at *eleven* last night. They have to advise me whenever a security report is filed for an attendee, including staff. How bad is it?" She glanced down at my hand as Gretchen returned to her desk.

I held up my pinky.

"What's going on?" Gretchen asked.

"Caity burned her finger."

They both had to squint to see the faint pink mark. How could it have hurt so bad and now looked like nothing, making *me* look like a total wimp?

"Nigel gave me some honey, and it worked wonders. A great anti-inflammatory."

Blair nodded vaguely. "I'm going to have you help out with registration this morning. Most of the international flights get in early, so the desk will be slammed until noon."

Why the hell couldn't Chad help out at registration? He was only in charge of four meeting rooms, and the meetings hadn't even started yet. The program kicked off tonight with a welcome reception, and I wasn't even sure what time it started. Gretchen would rip me to shreds.

"I haven't had time to review the event orders," I blurted.

Gretchen look surprised by my concern over the BEOs, and Blair looked miffed that I was questioning her decision to stick me at the registration desk.

"Gretchen's got things under control in the F and B world."

Gretchen's jaw tightened. "I planned to have Caity shadow the minibar attendant again. There are a lot more rooms checking in today."

"As long as it's the same guy doing it, it'll be fine. She gave him direction yesterday."

Gretchen's lips pressed into a thin line, like she was struggling not to speak her mind. Her mouth relaxed slightly. "I'll need Caity in the ballroom by three to help." She gave Blair a pointed look.

Blair shrugged. "Of course. Everyone will have checked in by then. There may be a few *challenges* with registration, so best to have an extra body this morning."

According to Rita, it was going to be a "bloody nightmare."

Wanting desperately to sneak back to my room and crawl into bed, I went in search of Nigel and an energy drink. I found the banquet captain in our breakfast room, talking to Armando, who avoided my gaze, rearranging scones on a platter.

Nigel joined me. "How is your finger?"

"Great." I needed to put on a Band-Aid so if people asked about it, I wouldn't have to show them it looked fine. Wanting to change the subject, I requested an energy drink.

"Did your injury keep you up late?"

"No, I was up helping two women research their ancestry before they visit Scotland this summer."

He arched a curious brow. "You're a genealogist?"

I shrugged. "An amateur. I dabble in my Irish ancestry."

Nigel's face lit up, and he looked almost giddy. "Might I hire you to assist with some family research? My mother took one of those DNA tests and has been devastated ever since. It claims she's only twenty percent English, rather than a hundred percent, as she always believed. The results showed she was also French and German. I'm the only person she has shared the information with. She won't even tell her dearest friend."

"I've read those tests can vary, and you inherit different amounts of DNA ethnicity from each parent."

"Family lore has it that my grandfather, who never knew his father, came from royal blood."

"What if I discover you have a connection to Louis the Sixteenth rather than Queen Victoria? You're okay with that?"

"I promise not to take off your head." He winked. "Her birthday is in May. Would be the perfect time to show her written proof our family tree is indeed of strong English descent. Please consider it. I'd be most appreciative."

I'd hoped to finish up Bernice and Gracie's research this month so I could start on my Flannery tree. I could feel for Nigel, wanting to solve his family's mystery. However, my Flannerys might have come from royal blood, but I'd never know it at this rate. Yet, I could use the extra cash after I'd forked out all that money on stack dolls. And I needed to pay for my international health insurance.

"I'll see what I can find out," I said.

"Splendid." Nigel went off to grab me an energy drink.

Armando rearranged sugar packets in a bowl while I checked the buffet. Nigel returned with a thick pea-green-colored liquid in a tall glass.

My top lip curled back. "What is that?"

"Enough energy to have you zipping around all day."

"A sixteen-hour day?" I took a sip of the slimy sludge that tasted like seaweed after it'd washed ashore and lay rotting on driftwood for months. "What is this?"

"A mix of kale, broccoli—"

I held up a halting hand. "Never mind. I'm better off not knowing."

"It's what keeps me going. That and the loo on the lower level."

"The loo?"

"It's located down a remote hallway where the meeting rooms aren't often utilized. When I need to get away from the madness, I hide out in the loo."

Nigel seemed too refined to be hiding out in bathroom stalls, precisely why he probably did it. Nobody would ever think of looking for him there.

"Where exactly is that loo?"

A bathroom stall might be my new Zen Zone.

After hours at the registration desk, my head was about to explode. People were firing questions at me nonstop.

The bellman took my luggage a half hour ago. Where is it?

The restaurant doesn't offer vegan options. Can you talk to the chef?

Where's the nearest pharmacy? I think I contracted something on the plane! The man about hacked up a lung while I scrambled for a pharmacy address. It turned out he wasn't even with our group. He'd wandered over from the lobby. I'd scrubbed myself down with antibacterial gel.

It finally started slowing down early afternoon, giving us our first breather.

"I can't believe we only had three people without rooms." Rita gave Courtney a pat on the back. "You did a fab job."

"We did a fab job. Sorry you got pulled into the mess." Courtney's pink shirt was untucked, most of her makeup was worn off, and only one gold earring dangled from her ear.

I wasn't sure if she'd lost the other one or had forgotten to put it in. Neither Rita nor I mentioned it, not wanting a missing earring to be the final straw that sent the poor thing over the edge.

"No worries, luv. It's not the first time, and it won't be the last. It could be worse. Last year I was on a meeting where the rooms' coordinator released two hundred rooms in error from a thousand-room block. There was a citywide convention, and hotels were sold out. Staff had to double up, and we were on every hotel booking website grabbing hotel rooms as they became available. Half the time they were in the next town over."

That woman had some horrific stories.

I sniffed the faint scent of lavender lingering on my suit jacket. I excused myself and escaped to Nigel's loo hideout on the lower level to take a break. When I entered the bathroom, the scent of vanilla calmed me. The cleaning lady was just leaving, a can of vanilla air freshener on her cart.

I pointed to the can. "May I?"

She looked confused but nodded okay.

I blasted the air with the vanilla scent and stepped through the mist, inhaling a deep breath. I stuck the can back on her cart. She gave me a wary smile and quickly wheeled her cart out the door before I could offer her 100 korunas for the air freshener.

CHAPTER TWELVE

Midafternoon, I finally scarfed down a few bites of lunch—cold goulash, dried-out mashed potatoes, and shriveled-up peas. It was probably delish when it had been hot and fresh. I grabbed my event order and went to the ballroom to help Gretchen with the welcome reception setup.

Crystal chandeliers hung from the brightly painted frescoed ceiling, and gilded wall sconces cast a soft light against the walls. Gold linens with champagne tulle overlays draped the tables. It resembled a ballroom at the Palace of Versailles. I snapped a few quick pics to post on Facebook, since this would likely be the only historical building I'd get to see the inside of this trip.

Gretchen was in food and beverage diva mode, firing off commands at Nigel and his staff, who were decked out in black suits with gold bow ties. Gretchen had changed into black heels, her hair was pulled back in a stylish twist, and she smelled like freshly spritzed designer perfume.

I smelled like the loo on the lower level.

Gretchen pointed a pen at me. "Caity, I'm putting you in charge of the dessert. *Ethan Hunt.* I'll handle everything else. You just focus on that."

A guy in jeans and a Grateful Dead T-shirt strolled up, twirling a drumstick between his fingers. "I'm here to set for the Chain-Smoking Altar Boys."

Gretchen's horrified gaze narrowed. "The what?"

He slid a hand through his greasy hair. "The band for tonight."

Her gaze darted to Nigel. "I contracted a trio."

Nigel nodded. "This gentleman is performing here in two nights. Not this evening."

The guy's brow wrinkled, and he stopped twirling the drumstick. "You sure about that?"

"Sadly, yes, I am quite certain your musical group will be here to entertain in two nights."

"Where the hell is security?" Gretchen's gaze darted to the doors. "Product is going out. They need to guard the doors."

Nigel had a server escort the Grateful Dead guy out of the room while Gretchen called security.

"I swear to God, if tonight doesn't go smoothly, I'm going to flip my shit," Gretchen said.

"Well, we certainly don't want that to flip." Nigel wore a strained smile, turning to me. "I'll help you retrieve the product from the cooler and set the dessert station."

"We cannot run out of dessert," Gretchen said. "This is their featured product. They sent like a hundred extras." Her gaze flew across the room. "Don't light those candles yet!"

The startled server dropped the lit match on the round mirror centerpiece displaying the candles, just missing the gold tulle and igniting the table.

"Be careful!" Gretchen yelled.

Nigel's jaw tightened. His gaze sharpened. Fearing that his unflappable demeanor was about to become ruffled, I grabbed hold of Nigel's arm and led him toward the refrigerator to cool off.

Fifteen minutes later, we were arranging macarons on three-tiered china stands painted with delicate gold borders and floral designs. The coffee and tea station displayed matching cups and saucers. The china looked like pieces Nigel would have inherited from an English grandmother or the hotel restaurant used to serve high tea.

"This china reminds me of the first time I met my Irish rellie this past Christmas. We drank tea from cups that came from my great-grandma Flannery's family porcelain factory. It's part of my growing teacup collection."

"Well then, we must add one more to your collection." Nigel handed me a dainty cup and saucer. "It was made in the former Czechoslovakia."

"Oh wow. Thank you." I wrapped it in a cream-colored linen and carefully tucked it inside my purse for safekeeping.

We finished placing out the desserts. Macarons were all the rage right now, but these were much fancier than your average ones. Champagne and raspberry, salted caramel praline, chocolate ganache sprinkled with nuts, lavender and white chocolate... Lavender? The VIP with the Zen suite would be all over those. I placed the dessert menu cards on the gold tulle and stored two extra boxes of product under the table.

Nigel and I stood back and admired our work.

"Fit for the queen," he said.

Gretchen walked up and studied the display. Unable to find a flaw, she smiled faintly. "Looks good." She continued to the pasta station.

A sense of pride welled up inside me. I scolded myself for allowing Gretchen's approval to evoke such a feeling. "That's the first compliment she's ever given me."

Nigel smirked. "I'll send some champagne to your room." He went off to round up the servers for a quick powwow before the doors opened.

My purse strap was pressing down on my bruised shoulder, so I stashed it under the table by the product. The aroma of hot appetizers on the next station made my stomach growl. Gretchen was across the room at the carving station, probably directing the chef on the proper way to slice the meat. I snuck over to the appetizers and snatched up a mini crab cake and a puff pastry with goat cheese. Starving, I choked down the stinky cheese. I returned to my post to find Armando— the server who'd gone MIA at my VIP dinner—perusing the desserts. I eyed his mouth. Were those macaron crumbs on his lips?

"Can I help you?" I asked.

He shook his head. Before I could hold out my hand and tell him to spit out the evidence, he bolted.

If Nigel caught Armando eating off a client's buffet, he'd fire him on the spot. It would be like a restaurant waiter snitching some of your dessert before delivering it to your table. I technically wasn't supposed to be eating off a buffet until after the event when I was no longer working. However, I was rarely not on duty, so when was I supposed to eat?

A few minutes later, Oscar—the server who'd come to my rescue at the dinner—walked up with a silver tray of rumaki. The scent of bacon filled my head. Gretchen was still on the other side of the room, so I popped a bacon-wrapped water chestnut into my mouth. I smiled thank you, and Oscar strolled over to the doors where Nigel was lining up servers to tray-pass wine and appetizers. A lady seated with a cello poised between her legs and two men, one with a viola and one with a violin, began playing on a low-rise stage at the front. Their black attire against the red velvet pipe-and-drape backdrop added to the elegance. Like the wineglass musician's tune on the bridge, I recognized the classical piece but didn't know the composer or title.

The doors opened. People dressed in dark suits and cocktail dresses flowed in, making a beeline for the bars. I didn't see much action until an hour into the reception when the desserts got hit fast and furious. A middle-aged lady in a black dress with a faux-diamond-embellished neckline browsed the macarons. Her name badge read Andrea Callan. The mental health VIP. As I'd expected, Zen Lady went wild for the lavender and white chocolate macarons. She wrapped several in a napkin and discreetly slipped them into her purse.

It wasn't my place to remind her that employees were informed that all product must remain in the function rooms.

Mr. Gauthier strolled over. My heart raced.

Do not screw up.

His top lip curled back at the lavender and white chocolate macarons. *"Est-ce correct?"* He pointed at the dessert, questioning if he was reading the flavor right.

I nodded. *"Oui."*

He snatched up a champagne raspberry one and walked off.

I let out a relieved sigh over our interaction having gone smoothly.

There were only twenty macarons left when there was finally a lull in traffic, allowing me time to replenish. I lifted the table linen to grab the extra product.

No boxes. I checked the other side. Still no boxes.

My heart raced.

Where the hell were the macarons?

And why had someone swiped the dessert and not my purse? No time? Or they knew my pathetic financial situation?

I'd left the station for five minutes to pee while Chad had kept an eye on it and when I'd popped over for appetizers, twenty feet away. Otherwise I'd been there all night, chatting with attendees and servers. Had it been swiped when I'd been talking with someone? Like a tag team of thieves? Who'd seen me stash the boxes under the table? Security had been at the main doors since the Grateful Dead guy was kicked out.

Gretchen was making her rounds, checking the station next to me. My stomach tossed. She was going to "flip her shit" when I told her about the missing product. Did I have to tell her? As far as she knew, we'd had a run on macarons and they were almost gone. But what if I lied and the product showed up somewhere down the road, like in competitor packaging on a food hall's shelf? Would they be able to trace it back to me?

What would Rachel do if she were in this situation?

She'd fess up and take responsibility, even though it really wasn't my fault.

Gretchen walked up, clipboard in hand. "What's on your badge?"

I glanced down to find teriyaki sauce from the rumaki had dripped on my plastic name badge holder. I wiped it off with my jacket sleeve. I had bigger things to worry about than being busted for eating while on duty. I told Gretchen about the missing boxes. I didn't mention that I'd left the station to sneak appetizers that weren't being tray-passed but admitted having made a loo run.

Panic filled her eyes. "How the hell did someone steal the boxes if you were here the entire time?"

"I have no clue."

She checked under the table. "Maybe you put them under the wrong table." She headed over to the pasta station.

Did she think I was a complete idiot?

The only thing Gretchen found under the pasta station's table was the chef's feet. "Guard what's left of the desserts," she said. "I'll check under every table." She waved Nigel over and filled him in on the situation, recruiting his assistance. "We're searching everywhere before I tell Blair that Caity lost the product."

"I didn't *lose* it. It was stolen."

Gretchen rolled her eyes. "Whatever. It's gone."

She searched under every food station, and Nigel discreetly put out an all-points bulletin to his staff.

A few minutes later, Oscar walked up and I snatched a piece of rumaki off his tray and popped it into my mouth, and then another. I had nothing to lose at this point.

"You know things have been disappearing lately," he said in a mysterious manner. "A vase and a sculpture vanished from the Presidential Suite. Only one housekeeper will even enter the room."

One housekeeper was responsible for cleaning that huge suite seven days a week? Great. Mindy and I would probably be changing Mr. Gauthier's sheets and cleaning his toilet.

Oscar walked off as Chad strolled past with appetizers piled on a plate, stuffing his face while I was in meltdown mode. He was going in for the last few macarons.

I snapped a hand out in front of the dessert stand. "Sorry. They're almost gone." Maybe Chad had looked under the table when the macarons were running low. "You didn't happen to replenish them when you were watching the buffet, did you?"

He shook his head.

I left it at that since I wasn't sure if I should tell staff what had happened.

"Guess I'll take more foie gras." He waltzed back over to the previous station.

Here was the thing. Zen Lady had stashed lavender macarons in her purse. Who was frisking her at the door? What was to stop attendees from smuggling out product? How well was Ted's security team policing the main doors? Granted, two boxes would be obvious, yet still. Someone could have snuck out a side door.

Gretchen and Nigel returned from scouring the kitchen, back hallways, garbage bins, even the boxes awaiting the trash compacter.

"We have to tell Blair," Gretchen said with a sense of dread. "Luckily, the reception finishes in fifteen minutes. Take away the empty dessert stands so people aren't asking for more."

Gretchen and I waited in a dingy back hallway for Blair. The stench of dirty dishes on overflowing busing trays about made me gag. Gretchen was texting away, so I checked e-mail to find one from George Wood. He'd arrived at his friend's home in Prague. I wanted to ask if his friend had an extra guest room, in case I got fired. I certainly couldn't afford to stay at Le Haute Bohème on my own dime.

Blair flew through the side doors. "What's going on?"

Gretchen gave her the skinny on the situation.

Blair's wild-eyed gaze narrowed on me. "How the hell did you lose two boxes of product? If you couldn't keep track of it, you should have left it locked up in the cooler."

Had this woman been named after the *Blair Witch Project*? Except the movie had come out in the late nineties.

"I'm sorry," I said. "I didn't want to run out of it. I thought it was better to have it on standby than having to wait for Nigel to bring it."

"Well, obviously it wasn't." She clenched her teeth. "I can't believe you lost product."

"I didn't *lose* it. Someone stole it."

"You shouldn't be hiding it under the table." Blair pressed her fingers to her temples. "Well, this is certainly the *challenge* of the day. Of the program, I hope."

"We hide stuff under tables all the time," Gretchen snapped. "Even you do." Her piercing gaze *challenged* Blair to deny it.

Blair looked shocked that Gretchen dared confront her. I couldn't believe Gretchen was coming to my rescue after she'd also just blamed me for losing the product. Her frustration with Blair was apparently greater than her frustration with me. I didn't blame Gretchen for being bitter that Blair took advantage of her expertise and abilities by not giving her support.

"It had to have been the hotel staff," Blair said. "Find out which one of them saw you put it under the table— that person must have swiped it. Get it back. Maybe I won't even have to tell the client."

How about Mr. Gauthier? Would she confide in him?

"If I lose my job over this, everyone loses their jobs." She stalked back into the ballroom.

Gretchen's face reddened with anger. "We all stash crap under tables, in cupboards, behind screens. I've seen Blair do it a dozen times. Not that she'd ever admit it. She thinks she's so perfect even though she doesn't know shit about meeting planning, especially food and beverage, which is why I never have help. I told her I wouldn't do this meeting without support. I should just walk out and see how she handles it."

I wouldn't handle it well. I couldn't do food and beverage by myself.

"I'm sick of not being appreciated," she said.

"I appreciate you sticking up for me even after you saw Declan here." My heart raced. I couldn't believe I'd just brought that up. Talk about adding fuel to the fire. But I'd felt pressured to be sympathetic and thankful so she didn't bolt.

Gretchen's jaw dropped. Her gaze narrowed. "Declan was here?"

She hadn't seen him getting into the taxi?

I nodded faintly, my stomach clenching.

"Good luck with that. You know it violates our contract to have guests stay over during a meeting." A warning look flashed in her eyes, and she marched back into the ballroom.

Rather than freaking out that Gretchen was off to tell Blair about Declan, I wanted to yell out, *Go right ahead. Put me out of my misery!*

Yet I couldn't afford to be put out of my misery.

CHAPTER
THIRTEEN

"How many Evans and Walker meetings have you worked?" Ted, the security guy, asked me.

"This is my first one."

"Have you worked with Taylor Made Events before?"

"No."

He stopped scrawling notes on his pad, glancing up with a curious look. "Who hired you?"

"Blair."

"Who referred you to her?"

"Declan Grady."

"How long has he worked for the company?"

"I don't know. You'd have to ask Blair."

And should I hire a lawyer?

Not only was I thought incompetent, but also a thief?

I maintained eye contact with Ted, trying not to fidget with the gold tulle on the table or to look guilty.

Because I wasn't guilty!

"So the thief took the product but left your purse?"

"Yes." I'd told him that three times. I picked up my purse for emphasis, then dropped it on the table. Crap. My teacup. I unzipped the purse and unwrapped the cup to make sure the fragile china hadn't broken.

Ted eyed my purse, then the dirty teacups waiting to be cleared from the table. "Is that a hotel cup in your purse?"

My heart raced. "I didn't swipe it. The banquet captain gave it to me."

He arched a skeptical brow, jotting down notes.

My gaze darted around the room for Nigel to corroborate my story, but he was nowhere to be found. I also hadn't stolen those prints from the guy on the street. I'd gotten them for free!

"Registration hasn't had to make any new badges, and we haven't had any lost ones turned in," Ted said. "So nobody unauthorized accessed the room." He eyed my badge.

Things could be worse. I could have lost my badge again, enabling the thief to steal the product while impersonating me.

After Ted's interrogation, I was mentally drained, yet determined to prove my innocence. I hunted down Nigel and posed similar questions about his banquet staff.

"I guarantee my staff would not jeopardize their positions or this hotel by stealing the product." He looked offended by my accusation.

"Everyone is a suspect. Even me. I was just questioned by security, as I'm sure you will be."

Armando was removing chafing dishes from the

appetizer station. He'd been skulking around the macarons, likely taste testing them.

"What about Armando? He was ticked that I contacted you when he went missing from my VIP dinner." The guy had been on a smoking break rather than addressing the dinner issues, and he'd eaten off a client's dessert station. He didn't appear concerned about keeping his job.

Had he been pissed enough to try to get me fired?

"He can be a bit lazy at times, but I truly don't think he's a thief." Yet Nigel's suspicious gaze narrowed on Armando. "However, rest assured I'll investigate." He marched off.

I'd just moved to the top of Armando's shit list.

If a hotel employee had swiped it, they'd likely handed it off to someone immediately and it was no longer in the hotel.

"It's never a dull moment, is it?" Mindy said, walking up. "I once had a VIP's suitcase go missing after it was given to the bellstand for delivery."

"How'd you find it?"

"We didn't."

"That's not very reassuring."

"Sorry. I'm sure we'll find this product. We should offer a reward. Some of these banquet guys look shifty, like they'd rat out their coworker for a few korunas."

I nodded. "Definitely an idea."

"Too bad they don't allow their company photographer at these product launches. He's so annoying—he'd definitely have gotten something on film. And there are no security cameras in this ballroom. But don't worry. We'll find the thief. I have a client who does those murder mystery trains all the time, and I'm always the first to figure out the murderer. Let's think...what would someone's motive be for swiping it?" She tapped a finger against her pink lips, her gaze narrowing. "Revenge, money...love..."

"A love of macarons?"

Her eyes widened. "Revenge. Mr. Gauthier. He was passed up for a huge promotion last fall. I heard him bitching about it on his cell while I was waiting to stick him in a sedan to the airport. He was furious. I had no clue what he was saying, but a bellman translated the gist of it."

"What's he going to do? Sell it on the black market?" Gretchen had mentioned corporate espionage. And Prague was the perfect setting for a spy thriller. Yet this was more like *Miss Marple and the Missing Macarons* than *Mission Impossible*.

Mindy's face lit up. "His buddy Mr. Blanchet went to work for a competitor last summer. They were inseparable. Maybe they've had this planned since he left. It's totally plausible. Motivation, means... He could have snatched it from under the table and slipped out the side door with it. We need to search his room."

If Mindy was willing to go in the haunted suite, she must really believe he was guilty, or wanted him to be. Did she know about Blair and him? Did she think if he got canned, Blair would be gone? *We'd* be gone if we pointed the finger at Blair's lover whether he was guilty or not.

"We can't search his room," I said. "Besides being wrong, if it was him, I'm sure he's already smuggled it out of the hotel."

He'd passed by the dessert station several times. He might have been in with the crush of people that swarmed the table at once. Had his lack of enthusiasm about the macarons been a ploy to throw me off his track?

Mindy shook her head, a pensive look on her face. "He wouldn't go to the length of stealing it, then hand it off to some random courier or someone who could possibly sell it for more. No, he still has it. Maybe Mr. Blanchet is in town and they're meeting right now in a deserted alley behind an absinthe bar."

What if we got caught rifling through this man's room? Yet what if he had taken it? Every problem with this meeting seemed to circle back to Mr. Gauthier.

And me.

❧ ☙

I dropped my computer bag on the guest room desk with a thud. If I were going to break into a VIP's suite, it was going to be Ms. Callan's so I could douse myself in her lavender air freshener. I took the china teacup and saucer from my purse and placed it next to Grandma's pic on my nightstand. Maybe Nigel giving me the teacup was a sign that Grandma was watching over me. That I wasn't alone in this mess.

I needed her sense of courage now more than ever.

Grandma had given up her family to be with the man she'd loved. Survived his death in a foreign country. And sailed alone across the Atlantic to an unknown land. My life could be a lot rougher, even though it didn't seem like it right now.

A text chimed on my phone. Mom.

How did the visit with George Wood go? Any new info?

We're meeting tomorrow night.

Keep me posted. Love, Mom.

Glad she was curious about our visit.

I FaceTimed Declan. As usual, I was calling from my guest room, whereas he was at a cool off-site event. He and attendees were strolling through an art-lined hallway in an old villa. He was decked out in a black suit and a five o'clock shadow, looking like an ad for his intoxicating cologne. I hadn't had the energy to even comb my hair.

I explained my bleak situation in a nutshell.

His smile vanished, and he stepped out of a set of French doors onto a terrace. "Who do you think nicked it?"

"Mindy suspects a VIP, Mr. Gauthier. Cricket guy. Did you know he's sleeping with Blair?"

"I hadn't heard that but don't doubt it. I know him to see him, but I've never worked with their VIPs."

"She wants to search his room. I told her no way. That's not right. Is it?"

"Not if you get caught. You'd definitely get the sack."

"I think I've already sealed my fate for future employment with this company. Hopefully, I haven't sealed yours. Security interrogated me, and I had to tell him you'd recommended me. Can you believe I'm a suspect?" I gasped. "What if I'm found guilty? They couldn't put me in jail here, could they? Omigod, remember that American woman who was imprisoned in—"

"You're not going to get thrown in jail." Declan's confident look reinforced his tone. "You're not guilty."

My heart raced. "What if I'm used as the scapegoat?"

"Ya won't be. You had no reason for stealing it, and there's no evidence. You'll get this straightened out. Especially with Mindy on your side. She can be fierce."

"Surprisingly, Gretchen kind of stuck up for me. That was before I mentioned you were here. She hadn't seen you get in the taxi."

"Feck." Declan dropped his head back, letting out a frustrated groan. "Sorry 'bout that. I was sure she'd been looking right at me when I hopped in the taxi. But it was a bit dark on the curb. She won't turn on ya, professionally anyway. She was in charge of the reception and the product."

"There's a server who doesn't like me much and might have stolen it just to spite me. I don't get it. I only left the table for five minutes while Chad watched it."

Declan rolled his eyes. "Jaysus. Chad's on his way out. Gretchen mentioned it when we were in Greece last fall. He's been getting a bit of an attitude and lazy, always on his mobile. Blair is tired of dealing with it."

Actually, Chad had *offered* to man the dessert station. I hadn't asked him.

"So maybe he did it for revenge," I said.

Declan shrugged. "Even good guys turn bad when they're desperate."

I collapsed onto the bed. "Tell me a story." I sounded like a little girl being tucked into bed at night. But Declan's stories always made me feel better.

Declan passed by a gazebo with ornate columns and a fancy mosaic-tiled dome, likely used for weddings. "Right, then. I've got one. When I was escorting a group in Salzburg, we took *The Sound of Music* tour, visited the von Trapp house. I made the mistake of admitting having seen the movie dozens of times thanks to Zoe's obsession with it. She used to make me sing the part of Rolf in 'Sixteen Going On Seventeen.' So when we were in the gazebo, the group convinced me to sing both parts and reenact the scene. An attendee filmed it on his mobile, and it ended up in the meeting's candid video clips played during closing session."

I laughed, picturing Declan as the young girl Liesl, twirling around the gazebo, leaping from bench to bench.

Someone called out to Declan, and he acknowledged them with a wave. "Sorry. Gotta run. Everything will be grand." He gave me a reassuring smile. "Love you."

Funny how just two words could make me feel like everything would be okay.

"Love you too, Liesl."

He quirked a brow. "Going to regret telling ya that story, aren't I now?"

I gave him a sly smile, and we said good-bye.

Talking to Declan made me feel better, but I really needed a hug...and a kiss...

A knock sounded at the door.

I peeked out the peephole to find a bellman holding a white wicker basket filled with items.

I left the security chain on and opened the door a crack. "Can I help you?"

"A room amenity for you, madam."

"I'm not supposed to receive group amenities."

I'd learned my lesson about gift basket protocol on my first meeting, after I'd pilfered a food and wine basket mistakenly delivered to my room.

He looked confused. "Compliments of Nigel, madam."

I undid the chain and opened the door.

He handed me the basket. "Enjoy." He marched off.

I set the heavy basket on the end of the bed. It contained a luxurious hotel-logoed robe. No more wearing the sketchy one in my closet. A candle, shower gel, body lotion, pillow spray, and a slew of other items in the hotel spa's signature scent, Seaside Escape, rather than the strong-smelling eucalyptus products in my bathroom.

I opened the card.

Thought you might like to escape to the beach.
Nigel

Had he recognized the vanilla air freshener scent, from his loo hideaway, on my suit?

I slipped on the robe and snuggled into its velvety softness. I spritzed myself with the pillow spray, a fresh, relaxing scent. I briefly escaped to a deserted island before I called Rachel and returned to harsh reality, recounting my story, *Miss Marple and the Missing Macarons.*

"It never fails," she said. "There's no such thing as a drama-free meeting. But don't beat yourself up. This could have happened to a seasoned planner. Hell, I'd have stashed the product under the table knowing I wouldn't have had time to get more. And if someone was determined to steal it, they'd have broken into the cooler if they had to."

"Gretchen said the same thing."

"See, she's not a total wench."

"Okay, she's ninety-five percent wench." Actually, this meeting she'd only been around eighty percent. Maybe that was because Blair was two hundred percent, making it relative. "And don't you dare call and tell her to stick up for me. She already thinks the only reason you hired me was because I'm your sister." In Dublin, she'd made a snide remark about picking up the slack for another planner's relative on-site and made it clear she wasn't going to pick up mine.

"That first meeting must have been rough on you. I'm sorry I wasn't more supportive. I'm glad Declan had your back."

Rachel's apology surprised me. And she rarely had anything positive to say about Declan on a personal basis since we'd started seeing each other.

"Thanks."

"You've come a long way, Caity. Don't let this planner shake your confidence. You're great at solving mysteries. You uncovered Grandma's history and tracked down Sadie Collentine. You'll figure this out."

My sister's confidence in me gave me hope. Having earned her respect meant a lot to me. She was right. I loved playing supersleuth when it came to genealogy research, but not when it came to saving my job and my butt from being thrown in jail.

"George Wood is in Prague. I hope to have time to meet him tomorrow night with this whole fiasco going on."

"Make time. You'll regret it if you don't. Just be sure to let someone know where you're meeting him."

Did Rachel regret all the times she'd chosen work over her personal life? She was right. I had to make time. I was too intrigued not to.

"In five years, you won't even remember tonight," she said. "So much other crap, probably even worse, will have happened."

Even worse? That wasn't comforting.

CHAPTER
FOURTEEN

Despite only having a few hours of restless sleep, the following morning I was running on pure adrenaline, determined to clear my reputation and capture the thief. Rather than lying in bed all night fearing I might be doomed, I pulled up the link that Nicholas Turney had sent me for James McKinney's military paper. It'd taken me an hour to decipher the fancy penmanship. The document noted his approximate birthdate was 1821 and he was from Paisley, a suburb of Glasgow, Scotland. Unfortunately, the papers didn't note his parents' names. However, they mentioned that he was tried and found guilty for having been drunk while on guard duty. Bernice and Gracie had said they didn't want to know anything horrible, like if their ancestor had been a murderer. However, he hadn't been dishonorably discharged—he'd been demoted in rank. Considering that the women loved their whiskey, they probably wouldn't judge James McKinney too harshly.

Having immigrated to Canada with the military,

he'd likely left his family behind. I had no clue how to trace the McKinneys forward in Scotland, but I was still inspired by my find.

I popped into the office to drop off my computer bag before joining Gretchen in the main breakfast room, where our staff now ate after the attendees. My stomach tossed at the thought of facing Gretchen and Blair. Gretchen because of Declan more so than the macarons. However, as upset as she was with Blair, I didn't see Gretchen narking on me for having had Declan stay over.

Chad was alone in the office, sorting boxes in his crisply ironed pink shirt and starched pink tie with white polka dots. The only time he appeared busy was when Blair might see him.

I gave him a smile rather than a suspicious glare. "So security's questioning was pretty intense last night, hey?"

He shrugged. "He just asked if I'd watched the desserts for you for a few minutes."

Why hadn't Ted drilled him with questions like he had me? Had he merely been verifying if I'd been telling the truth? If the rumor about Blair giving Chad the ax was true, shouldn't she be questioning his guilt? I wanted to ask her if she considered him a suspect, yet I couldn't tell her why I thought that or she'd know someone had leaked he was being let go. Maybe the theft hadn't been premeditated but Chad had seized the opportunity when I'd asked him to watch over the macarons.

"To think, someone might be paying millions on the black market for some stupid macarons," Chad said.

"Black market macarons." A devious smile spread across his face. "I'd be able to pay off my house and retire early."

Just the other day he'd been wondering how he was going to retire...

"Who would you sell them to?"

He rattled off several competitors, as if he'd been compiling a list.

"The drama gets exhausting sometimes." He held out a stack of sign inserts. "Could you put these in the signboards on your way to the breakfast?"

Chad managed his stress quite well by not giving a rip.

"Ah, sure."

"Thanks." He snatched up his phone and started texting.

Fuming that he hadn't slipped up and confessed, and that I was doing his work while he screwed off, I shoved the inserts in the signboards as I marched down the hallway toward breakfast.

I'd now officially worked every position on this meeting.

Ted's security guys were lined up at the ballroom's main entrance, guarding the closed doors. I glanced down making sure my stupid badge was still there. Before I went inside, I removed the Seaside Escape pillow spray from my purse and gave myself a blast, picturing Declan and me drifting along the Mediterranean on a private yacht...

Boring cream tablecloths had replaced the gold linens and tulle overlays, and the gold covers and bows had been removed from the standard red banquet chairs.

Rather than fancy food stations scattered throughout the room, three cream-skirted buffet stations ran down the center. The frescoed ceiling and ornate sconces still gave the room a castle-like feel. Gretchen was checking the expiration dates on milk cartons. Hotel staff were putting the finishing touches on the buffets, except for Armando, who stood chatting with Ted. The only thing Armando seemed attentive toward was the desserts, making me even more suspicious. No matter what dessert was being showcased this morning, I was eating at least two, maybe three. Ted's watchful gaze followed me across the ballroom to where I joined Nigel at the coffee station.

The doors still weren't open, so I poured a cup of hot water and added three tea bags and some honey to kill the bitterness.

"Thanks for the gift," I told Nigel. "My room smells like an island getaway." As did I.

"You're quite welcome. I didn't believe you'd have time to make it to the spa, so I thought it best to bring the spa to you." His chipper smile faded into a grim expression. "And still no clues on the missing product."

"I'm offering a two-thousand-koruna reward for any info." I'd just made that decision. It sounded like a ton of money but was only around a hundred bucks. Cheaper than bailing myself out of jail. "Maybe one of your staff heard or saw something but is afraid to come forward." I eyed Armando, straightening a cloth napkin at a place setting.

"I'm still on it. This is far from finished." Nigel snatched an envelope from a busing tray. "Here's everything we have on our Stanton family history."

The envelope contained four sheets of paper. Not a lot to go on.

"Photocopies?" I asked. "You certainly don't want to entrust me with original documents."

"I trust you. But yes, they are copies. Do you charge an hourly rate or a flat fee?"

"Ah, a flat fee."

"Will a three-hundred-dollar advance suffice?"

"A hundred is fine."

"Don't sell yourself short. What you lack in experience, you make up for in determination and passion. I can see the sparkle in your eyes when you talk about your research."

I smiled, appreciating the extra money, which would pay for the reward I was offering. I scanned his family tree. "Your grandparents were from Lancashire?"

He nodded. "Have an aunt still there."

"Her name's not Daly, is it?"

He arched a curious brow. "No. Why?"

Despite not wanting to get Nigel's hopes up that I was some genealogist whiz, I told him about the success I'd had with my Coffey research and about my meeting with George Wood tonight. It might help to have Nigel know about my clandestine activity at the café in case I needed him to cover for me. Or if I was abducted and didn't return, he'd know where I'd gone so everyone didn't merely assume I'd hopped a plane home.

Gretchen joined us and informed Nigel that soy milk was missing from the cereal station. He got right on it, marching off to the kitchen.

Gretchen's black winged eyeliner was outlined in

emerald green today. Her blonde hair was pulled back in a wavy updo. Seriously. What time did she get up? I wasn't even sure I'd combed my hair before throwing it up in a clip this morning. I had put on lip gloss and mascara—on both eyes, I hoped.

She eyed the envelope in my hand. "What's that?"

"Nigel's family history. I'm helping him with some research."

"Ancestry research?"

"Yeah. I researched my grandma Coffey's family."

She nodded. "That's right. We went to that Coffey pub in Dublin. How'd you know Nigel's interested in his family history?"

"It came up in conversation."

Gretchen looked baffled how such a personal topic would have come up, as her interaction with staff revolved around outdated milk cartons or runny eggs. Unless a banquet server screwed up, she never even knew the staff's names.

"I was telling him about my grandma's relatives I found in Ireland."

"You found *living* ones?"

I nodded. "And dead ones."

Gretchen arched an intrigued brow. Like maybe she'd always dreamed of locating the wretched woman who'd abandoned her as a baby on some random doorstep in a basket. I had to think Gretchen's nasty disposition was deeply rooted in childhood—and further fueled by work stress.

Her features softened. "My sister always talks about researching our dad's family. We know nothing about them. He died when I was ten."

Gretchen had a sister? Her dad had died when she was young? Sympathy tugged at my heart. A foreign and unnerving feeling when it came to Gretchen.

She opened her mouth, then snapped it shut, a torn look on her face. Did she want to ask me to help research her dad's family? No. Gretchen would never ask me for help. I couldn't believe she'd confided in me in the first place. This was too weird and getting weirder the longer we stood there in silence.

"What do you think about Chad?" I asked, changing the topic. "Could he have swiped the macarons while he was watching the table? He might have found out Blair isn't hiring him for future programs. Mindy mentioned an upcoming incentive trip in Monte Carlo, and he'd looked surprised, like he hadn't known about it. Maybe he realized he was out."

Gretchen's gaze narrowed. She assumed Declan was my source on Chad. "He wouldn't steal the product. However, he spends all his time texting or surfing the web, so someone could easily have swiped it while he was goofing off." She hesitated, then continued. "And you don't have to worry. I don't have a thing for Declan. I might have, but not anymore. I'm seeing someone." She plastered on a reassuring smile, overcompensating. "He's a friend. That's it. He's a tortured soul, and that'll never change."

Gretchen didn't know Declan had become a tortured soul when his wife, Shauna, died three years ago. In Paris he'd confided in me and sworn me to silence. I'd slipped up and told Rachel, which was how she'd discovered our relationship. It was a relief that we were no longer hiding it from Rachel or Gretchen.

Sneaking around made me feel like our relationship was wrong.

The doors opened, and attendees trickled in. Gretchen eyed the envelope in my hand, then headed over to greet people. I let out a relieved sigh, stashing Nigel's family history under the coffee station, hoping it didn't mysteriously disappear like the macarons.

A part of me—the crazy, insane part—debated offering to help Gretchen learn about her father's family. Could I afford to turn down a client?

Even if it was Gretchen?

CHAPTER FIFTEEN

Following breakfast, I saw Blair when the staff herded attendees into the opening session. I successfully avoided eye contact and felt an overwhelming sense of relief when the session started and she headed to the office. Mindy asked for my assistance with VIP room deliveries that Blair wouldn't entrust to the bellstand.

I told her about my delivery debacle in Paris. How the bellstand had picked up wineglasses without my knowledge when I'd forgotten to lock the office and delivered them without instructions. The gifts had ended up in the wrong rooms. Mindy and I laughed. I never thought I'd laugh about my mishaps. I was starting to feel like Declan with his stories.

Our last delivery was Mr. Gauthier's suite. It suddenly dawned on me. "You brought me with to help search his room, didn't you?"

"Now we have a valid excuse for being in there."

She must be hell-bent on proving this guy guilty if she was willing to enter the haunted suite.

"We can't search his suite."

"Please don't make me go in there by myself." Her blue eyes pleaded with me.

"You're afraid of ghosts, aren't you?"

"All right, I admit it. And I feel really shitty. I wasn't busy that night of the cricket. I was freaked out at the thought of going into the suite alone. I'm so sorry."

Mindy was to blame for Declan and me missing our romantic dinner? I couldn't believe she'd done that. I'd prefer to resent Blair. I was ticked. However, Mindy looked petrified every time she went near the suite. She was genuinely freaked out by ghosts, not merely trying to pawn her work off on everyone, like Chad. And I owed her one after the slipper incident.

"Fine, I'll go in with you if you tell me why you're so sure he's guilty."

Mindy's gaze sharpened. "Because he's always so holier than thou, acting like he's so much better than everyone when he's cheating on his wife with Blair, of all women. And he acts like I'm invisible. I doubt he even knows my name. His English isn't great, but he could still speak to me."

That made him guilty of poor taste in women, and lacking morals, but it didn't make him a thief. I had to admit, I thought less of the guy for having an affair with Blair when he'd always seemed nice to me.

"I'm not rifling through his undies drawer," I said. "And if we do find the missing product, how are we going to explain that to Blair?"

She shrugged. "It's not like we broke in. I also need to see if the extra hangers we requested are in the closet and if housekeeping cleaned the fridge. Stuff I didn't have time to double-check because he'd arrived earlier than expected. Besides, this guy had a private butler at a resort unpack his suitcase and pack his dirty clothes. He doesn't care if people see his personal stuff."

Well, I didn't want to see it.

Mindy took an encouraging breath, and we stepped inside the suite. We placed an expensive Bohemian crystal vase on the cocktail table in the living room, with a note advising him that the company's gift would be shipped to him, so he didn't have to pack it. Once Mindy stuck him in the car to the airport, she'd have to scurry back up to the suite and secure the display vase.

Luckily, he hadn't yet packed and housekeeping hadn't cleaned his room, since he was departing today. No cardboard boxes marked *Ethan Hunt* had been tossed in the garbage, and no macarons in the cleaned fridge. An eerie feeling crawled across my skin. I glanced around, feeling like I was being watched, more from guilt than a ghost.

Mindy walked out of the bedroom. "The safe is locked. I'd have to have engineering open—"

"Engineering is not opening his safe. That would definitely be an invasion of privacy. Even out of the boxes, the product wouldn't fit in the safe."

"Just because we didn't find it doesn't mean he didn't swipe it."

"What about Chad?" I said. "He watched the desserts while I ran to the bathroom."

"What would his motive be?"

I told her about Chad being on his way out.

"I heard that like a year ago, and he's still here." She shrugged. "But who knows. You know I'd have hidden the product under the table also. You can't feel bad about that."

As we were leaving the room, a bright light flashed. The black dots disappeared from in front of my eyes, and two guys came into focus. One was dressed in a camouflage jacket, the other in all black.

"Sorry about that." The camo guy had an American accent, craning his neck to see around me. "Just trying to get a picture of the haunted suite. Do you work here? Do you think we could sneak a peek?"

"No," Mindy snapped. "There's a guest staying in there."

"We wouldn't have to go inside..."

Mindy pointed down the hallway. "Leave or I'm calling security."

The guy pressed his hands out in front of him. "Relax."

They strolled off toward the elevators, shooting us nasty looks over their shoulders as they turned the corner.

"They'll be back," I said.

Mindy nodded. "Call Blair and have her put security on alert. I have a departure in ten minutes. As much as I'd like Mr. Gauthier to find out his sweetie pie stuck him in a haunted suite, I don't have the energy to deal with her crazy right now." Mindy took off down the hall.

I called Blair, who requested that I stay put and play bouncer. Security was busy. Mr. Gauthier would be back to his room after his presentation, to pack up and leave. Perfect. I could avoid Blair a bit longer. Hopefully, someone didn't call hotel security to report *me* lurking around outside the suite.

Since this would be my last visit to the room, I Googled the hotel's haunted history. Sasha Petrov—the daughter of a Russian vodka tycoon—had died in the suite where she was staying on the eve of her wedding. Her mother had found her. It was an unsolved yet suspicious death. She'd been nineteen years old.

Five years younger than me.

My gaze slid to the suite's door, a chill slithering up my back. Not only at the thought of this poor woman having been murdered on the other side of that door but also because the first time I'd entered the suite, I'd envisioned a man sipping a strong liquor, like vodka, while reading about prohibition in America. Sasha's parents? That was insane. Yet a part of me wanted to see if I could find a photo of them online...

Wait a sec. Petrov? Had this woman been related to Madam Petrov, Fritzie's mom? Possibly sisters? Both the dog and his master looked like they came from old money. Was that why she'd been coming to the hotel for over fifty years? Hoping to make contact with her sister's ghost? But then why wouldn't she stay in the Presidential Suite? Because our group already had it booked? No, it hadn't been part of our original room block. Interesting that Mr. Gauthier's random act of kindness had endeared him to both Madam Petrov and Fritzie.

Curious, I pulled up my Ancestry.com app to see if Sasha Petrov had a family tree mentioning a sister. When I didn't find one, I Googled the family. Sasha Petrov had had a younger sister, Natalya, who'd now be close to ninety, around Madam Petrov's age...

I searched for Sasha's death record, wondering how

she'd died. A kidnapping gone bad? Had her fiancé been involved?

The two inept yet determined ghost hunters were back, heading down the hallway toward me.

"We decided this is public space, so we can hang out here," the guy in the camouflage jacket said.

The other guy nodded. "Yeah, Caity, we're just gonna hang out." He gestured to the vending machine in the alcove. "Get some snacks." He held up his phone. "Watch *Ghostbusters*."

Great. Now these stalkers knew my name.

Mr. Gauthier headed toward us, wearing a dark suit and an air of confidence, a sense of urgency in his stride. He was running late.

My heart raced. "Here comes security. Just so you know, taking a picture of the inside of an occupied guest room is illegal here. So thanks for stopping back and saving him the trouble of having to hunt you guys down."

The guys exchanged panicked looks, then took off down the hallway, crossing paths with Mr. Gauthier.

I gave myself a mental pat on the back.

Mr. Gauthier peered over his shoulder at the guys disappearing around the corner. "Are you good?"

I nodded. "They were on the wrong floor."

I advised him that I'd be walking him to his car.

"That will not be necessary. But thank you for all of your assistance and efforts this meeting."

Efforts being my poor attempt at speaking French when most meeting staff probably didn't even make an effort with a *bonjour* or *merci*.

"My English, it is not so good."

"You're English is much better than my French."

He smiled. "You are too kind."

He entered his suite, and I ducked into the alcove with the ice machine, not wanting to leave my post until he was gone. Ten minutes later, he left with his suitcase. I texted Mindy a heads-up that he was on his way. If he had the evidence, it was now leaving the hotel. With any luck, Mindy wouldn't go off the deep end and tackle him to search his luggage. If she did, my gut told me she wouldn't find the missing product. That Mr. Gauthier was not the thief.

Then who was?

I reevaluated my short list of suspects as I headed toward the lunchroom to help Gretchen. I had to be missing a clue. Chad didn't seem motivated enough to go to the trouble of planning a theft. If it'd been spur of the moment, he didn't seem smart enough to not get caught. However, there were a lot of dumb thieves. Like the guy selling the prints out of the plastic garbage bag.

Speaking of incompetent, lazy employees, Armando was rearranging paper napkins on the coffee station when I entered the ballroom. He was definitely still a suspect.

"So your grandpa never knew his father?" Gretchen asked Nigel, sounding genuinely intrigued by his family history.

He shook his head. "According to family lore, his father was of royalty, and married. My mother would love to prove she has blue blood running through her veins, even if he was illegitimate."

Gretchen peered over at me. "Could you go get more product from the cooler? Ted needs to keep a watch on what's displayed, and his team is outside all the breakout rooms." She handed me the key.

She was so enthralled by Nigel's family history she was trusting me to get the product?

Nigel sent my buddy Armando to assist me.

Maybe my sense of doom and panic that first day in the iron-barred cage had been a premonition of what was to come. My involvement with the missing product, not me going to jail. Hopefully. After stacking five boxes on the server's cart, I turned to head out, tripping over two boxes. Why had someone set those in the middle of the floor?

Ethan Hunt was written on them in black marker.

Omigod. "The missing macarons," I muttered.

I shot Armando a suspicious look.

"What?" he said innocently, yet his face paled.

I snatched the boxes off the floor. "How did the missing macarons get back in the cooler?"

He shrugged. "Maybe you never took them out."

Ugh! He sounded like Gretchen.

"I took them out."

One box had been opened. I counted the product inside to find one missing. Great. I padlocked the cage and clutched the boxes against my chest as I marched toward the ballroom, Armando rolling his cart behind me. I made a beeline over to Gretchen, motioning Nigel to join us.

"Look what materialized in the cooler," I said.

Gretchen's eyes widened with surprise. "Thank God."

I couldn't believe she wasn't questioning if the boxes had been there the entire time, like Armando had.

"However, one piece is missing," I said.

Gretchen shook her head, rolling her eyes. "Figures."

"This is most disturbing," Nigel said. "Someone would have needed my key to access the cooler, which is kept in my office when I'm not here. I share my office with two coworkers. I can't guarantee the door has never been left unsecured. But I can assure you that I will get to the bottom of this."

I handed Gretchen our key, never wanting to be responsible for it again.

"Show Blair you found the product," Gretchen said.

I headed to the office, excited to clear my name. Blair was alone at her desk, madly typing away on her laptop. "I hope you haven't told the client about the missing macarons. I found them. Well, all but one piece. Actually, they found their way back to the cooler. And trust me—they weren't there last night."

Blair's dark-eyed gaze narrowed on the box. "One piece is still missing? I'm going to pretend like I didn't just hear that. Thank God I hadn't mentioned it yet. So it *was* someone with the hotel if they turned up in the cooler. Unless someone picked the lock."

I nodded. "And I'm going to figure out who."

"Have security destroy the product."

After all of that, I was having them destroyed?

"Nothing is being shipped back. Packaging doesn't need to be shredded, since it's generic. It's now security's problem."

Except finding the thief was still *my* problem.

This was far from over.

I marched back into the ballroom straight over to Ted and handed him the product.

"Where'd you find it?" he asked.

"In the cooler."

He eyed me with suspicion. "It just materialized in the cooler?"

"Yes, it did. Armando was with me when I found it."

His stern features relaxed slightly. "Doesn't matter. Meeting is done today. Just glad we got the product back."

"Yeah, it does matter. I'm not guilty. You need to find out who is so everyone knows I didn't do it." I needed more business from Blair's company even if I didn't care to work with her again. And I hoped the staff would recommend me for jobs.

He shrugged. "I fly out in the morning."

What happened to his secret-agent attitude?

"Aren't the local police going to want this solved?"

He shook his head. "We didn't involve them. Wanted it to stay under the radar."

I marched over to Nigel. "I'm raising the reward to three thousand korunas. Even though it won't do me any good if a ghost took the product."

He quirked an inquisitive brow. "Would a ghost be able to eat macarons?"

"What would a ghost need with a vase or a sculpture?"

Nigel's gaze narrowed with interest. "How did you know about those thefts?"

"Oscar." Now I'd have two servers out to get me. "Forget I said that. I didn't mean to get him in trouble."

"Oh, he's in trouble all right. Only upper management and security were aware of those thefts. And, of course, the thief."

Our gazes darted to Oscar. The kind server who'd snuck me rumaki and came to my rescue at the VIP dinner. Nigel and I marched over to the man, who gave us a cheery hello.

"Pray tell, how did you know about the theft of the Presidential Suite's vase and sculpture?" Nigel asked.

Oscar's smile vanished. "Someone told me."

"Who?" Nigel demanded.

Oscar's panicked gaze skittered back and forth while he scrambled for a response. When he couldn't come up with one, he took off across the ballroom, toward the back exit. Nigel and I raced after him.

"Stop him," I yelled out to Gretchen as the server was about to escape out the door.

Gretchen bolted in front of Oscar, and they collided. She fell on her butt. Oscar stumbled backward. As he regained his balance, I grabbed hold of the bottom of his suit jacket. He attempted to shrug himself free, his arms getting stuck in the sleeves behind his back. It was straight out of a cheesy whodunit TV show.

Ted raced over and secured the guy.

I got in Oscar's face. "Why'd you take the macarons?"

"I didn't take them," he said.

"Then why'd you run?" Ted asked.

"I was afraid nobody would believe me and I'd be blamed."

I could relate to that.

"Yes, he took them," Armando said. "And I saw him with the vase."

Oscar's face reddened with anger. "My pay is meager. I ask for a raise, and I never get it. I am one of the only staff who is not afraid of ghosts and will go into the haunted suite, yet no raise. It's not right."

"So why'd you put the macarons back?" Gretchen asked.

"Because I thought he saw me take them." Oscar gestured to Armando.

"Where's the missing piece of product?" I asked.

Oscar wore a sheepish expression. "I ate it."

"How can you prove you ate it and aren't going to sell it?" I said.

"Let's pump his stomach," Gretchen said.

Oscar gasped in horror.

My gaze darted to Gretchen. "Are you serious?"

She nodded, stepping toward the server. "I'll do it myself if I have to."

Oscar pulled a small silver package with the words *Ethan Hunt* from his jacket pocket and whipped it on the ground in front of Gretchen. She snatched it up with a sense of triumph.

"How did you know he still had it?" I asked. "Did you see it in his pocket?"

Gretchen shrugged. "I had no clue he had it. I was just pissed he'd eaten one and wanted to scare him."

I smiled at her. "Good job."

She nodded. "You too."

I glared at Oscar. "I can't believe you'd have let me take the fall for it." And that Armando hadn't been guilty.

Oscar shrugged without apology.

Nigel's gaze sharpened on Armando. "Why didn't you tell me all of this?"

"He is the director's son. But I just confirmed he's guilty. So I get the reward, right?" Armando asked eagerly.

I gave him an incredulous look. "No, you don't get the reward. You didn't come forward willingly with the info."

"*We* should get a reward," Gretchen said, gesturing to me.

"Yes, we should." I peered over at Nigel.

He gave us a palms up. "Sorry. Seeing as it was not public knowledge, there was no reward being offered. I would be more than happy to give you a sugar bowl and creamer set to match your teacup."

I shot Ted a victorious grin, having proven my innocence in both the macaron and teacup thefts.

CHAPTER
SIXTEEN

I finished work ten minutes before I was due to meet George Wood. A nervous feeling fluttered in my chest as I entered the trendy café filled with fashionably dressed locals and tourists. I brushed a hand down the front of my wrinkled suit jacket and over my name badge. I shoved the badge in my purse. I swiped clear gloss across my lips. The place was a major contrast to Le Haute Bohème and old-world Prague. Groupings of white leather button-tuck chairs and low-sitting couches surrounded purple plastic-molded cocktail tables. Purple leather stools lined a white bar with purple uplighting. At least there was no loud techno thumping music.

A short gray-haired man dressed in a preppy green sweater, a collared shirt, tan slacks, and a gray wool hat resting on his knee sat alone on a couch in a corner, looking out of place and quite uncomfortable. Based on his anxious gaze glued to the door, he was either waiting for a hot date or me. Any fear I had of being abducted by an online psycho vanished.

Our gazes met, and he pushed himself up from the couch, standing just a few inches taller than me. He greeted me with a warm smile and enveloped my hands in his, giving them a gentle squeeze, introducing himself.

I eyed the couch. "I'm so sorry. Would you like to go somewhere else?"

"Nonsense. This place is quite exquisite. And it's hopping." He had a casual appearance compared to Nigel, yet a refined air about him.

I sat on the couch, and he joined me.

"Thank you so much for meeting," he said.

"Thank you for taking the train over from Vienna. I'd love to travel by train in Europe sometime."

I'd once taken Amtrak from Milwaukee to Chicago for a shopping spree on the Magnificent Mile. The charges were probably still sitting on my credit card.

He fidgeted with the brim of his gray wool cap. "Ah, I must admit—I didn't take the train from Vienna. I flew in from England. I feared you might find it an odd thing to do, come this far to meet with you."

I found it *odd* he hadn't told me the truth from the beginning. Why had he lied? The nervous fluttering returned to my chest.

I managed a smile. "Not at all."

Flames shot up from the table next to us, startling me. A fire danced around inside two glasses with spoons resting across the tops. A woman snapped shots of her male companion pretending he was going to drink the flaming liquor. I took a pic. The waitress snuffed out the flames with a plate.

"Merely a show to impress the tourists," George said. "Not the traditional means for drinking absinthe."

"Sorry. I didn't realize this is an absinthe bar."

"Many Prague bars serve the liquor. Mostly to entice tourists, I'd think. I shall stick with a local hard cider."

He flagged down a waitress, and we both ordered cider, my preferred drink in Ireland.

We already had something in common.

Starving, I suggested an extensive array of appetizers, my treat. Besides working crazy long hours, I deserved a bonus for capturing the macaron thief.

"I can't wait to hear about my grandma and her husband John Michael Daly. Do you know where they lived?"

He nodded. "I do indeed." He removed an envelope containing pictures from his jacket pocket and handed it to me.

"Oh shoot, I have a photo of my grandma and her sister that I should have brought. I'll send you a copy."

Anticipation raced through me as I slipped the photos from the envelope. The top one was of a historical manor on a sprawling estate filled with massive trees and a fancy garden. Not quite as grand as Downton Abbey but larger than the Daly estate in Killybog. You could fit twenty of Grandma's humble Irish stone cottages into this stately home. I could picture her and John Michael on the lawn enjoying afternoon tea and a leisurely game of croquet. I'd like to believe that they'd finally found some peace together before he was taken so unexpectedly.

"This home is incredible," I said. "Does the Daly family still live there?"

"Yes, I've spent my entire life on the estate. You must visit sometime."

"Omigosh, I'd love to."

The Daly estate was now number one on my bucket list.

The next pic was of a gravestone. The inscription read John Michael Daly.

"What a beautiful grave."

The tombstone's statue was mesmerizing. A man with feathered wings fanned out from his back floated just off the ground, embracing a woman, about to kiss her for the last time. She was clinging to him, trying to prevent him from leaving. I envisioned it as Grandma having to let go of her husband after they'd fought all odds to be together. The only thing their love couldn't endure was death.

My eyes glassed over with tears.

"It is quite lovely, isn't it?"

I nodded.

It might sound crazy, and a bit morbid, but visiting my Coffey family graves in Killybog had been one of the highlights of my trip.

The waitress returned with our pints.

"Here's to new friends," George said.

We clinked glasses.

I took a sip of the familiar sweet apple taste, reminiscent of Flanagan's cider ale, a comforting feeling washing over me.

The next pic was a black-and-white one of Grandma and her husband dressed in the same outfits as their engagement photo. A couple stood next to them admiring the baby in Grandma's arms, dressed in a long white gown and cap.

"That was my christening," George said.

I glanced up at him. "My grandma was your godmother?"

He slowly shook his head, a sense of hesitation in his gray eyes. His breathing quickened, causing a faint whistling sound between his lips. He took a deep breath, and the whistling stopped. "No, she was actually...my biological mother."

My brow narrowed in confusion. "Your *mother*?"

He nodded. After taking a drink of ale, he took an encouraging breath. "I was raised by Isabella Daly and Henry Wood, my godparents in that photo. Before my mother Isabella passed away eight years ago, she shared a family secret kept for the duration of my life. That my parents were Bridget Coffey and my mother's cousin John Michael Daly."

My heart raced.

Grandma had another *child*?

Mom had a *half brother*?

I had a *half uncle*?

Maybe I'd take an absinthe after all.

"I see she never mentioned me." He sounded disappointed yet not surprised. "I had no siblings or close relatives to share the news with, merely my wife, Diana. So I was quite overjoyed when I received your reply confirming Bridget Coffey was your grandmother. When I learned of my real parents, I visited my father's grave but didn't know where to begin searching for my mother. Isabella had heard she'd immigrated to America. That was all she knew. I found her Ellis Island record, but"—his voice filled with emotion—"then her trail disappeared after that." George's eyes watered, and his cheeks flushed.

I placed a trembling hand gently on his.

"I'd like the chance to get to know my biological mother's family. I'm so glad we found each other."

My research hadn't impacted merely my immediate family's life, but also George's. His questions would have gone unanswered had I not happened upon that forum and posted a message four months ago.

George shifted on the couch, looking unnerved by my silence, rather than uncomfortable with his seating.

"You have her heart-shaped face," I said. "Like Rachel and me."

He smiled, massaging his jawline. "I often wonder how different my life would be had I been raised in Ireland or America."

Mine certainly would have been different if I'd been raised on an English estate. But I knew from *Downton Abbey* that even estates had financial troubles. Just because he lived in an elaborate historical home didn't mean he was wealthy. However, it certainly didn't appear to be in disrepair. It looked like it should be part of an English stately home and garden tour.

"Did you know her?" George asked. "Your grandmother?"

A text chimed on my phone, and I jumped.

You had to be kidding.

"Excuse me just a second," I said. "So sorry. I'm on call." I slipped the phone from my suit pocket. Blair.

All hands on deck in the office.

It was 9:00 p.m. I deserved a few hours off before I

took a nap and returned to work tomorrow morning. Besides, was I really on call 24/7? Once I was released for the day, shouldn't I be done? It wasn't like I got overtime pay or even a thank-you from Blair when I'd answered her crazy cricket text or her call to greet Mr. Gauthier when I'd been informed we had the night off. She'd said good night when we left the office tonight, so I planned to have a *good* one.

George peered anxiously at me. He'd waited eight years to learn about the mother he'd never known. I'd only waited two weeks for Declan's friend Peter to locate my Coffey rellies, and it had seemed like forever. I wasn't making George wait any longer.

If I didn't reply to Blair's text, I could later claim I'd been in a dead zone and hadn't received it for hours. Or did I tell the truth, that I'd had a family emergency? Either way, Blair would be ticked. So I decided to be honest. Maybe she'd respect that I'd told her the truth.

In middle of family emergency. I'm sorry.

I'd likely just sealed my fate for future business from Blair, her colleagues, and every planner she knew.

"If you must leave, I fully understand."

"No, I'm fine." Heart thumping, I turned off my phone. "Unfortunately, I was only seven when my grandma died, so I don't have a lot of memories, but the ones I do have are wonderful. My sister, Rachel, and I used to drink tea from a lovely teacup collection that lined Grandma's windowsills."

He relaxed back on the couch. "How very Irish of her."

"I recently discovered they were from her Flannery family's porcelain factory."

"Do you still have the collection?"

I nodded. "I'll e-mail you photos and you can select a few. I'll send them to you."

He smiled appreciatively. "That would be lovely."

"We used to wear her aprons while helping her bake. She made the best bread. Probably Irish brown bread and a family recipe, but we didn't know it at the time. It was dense, yet soft and crumbly, with a crunchy crust."

He closed his eyes, a contented smile on his face. "I can taste the bread as we speak. Do you still have the recipe by chance? My wife is quite the baker."

"My aunt does. We just learned about my grandma's Irish background a few months ago."

"You weren't aware she was Irish?"

"We were, but she never discussed her life in Ireland." I left out the part that she'd claimed her entire family in Ireland was dead, since that would also have included George. I didn't want the poor man to think that he'd been dead to her, and I didn't want to believe he had. I needed to believe she'd thought about him every day. "We never knew her relatives' names until she died and we found letters from her sister Theresa. My mom was pretty upset. After I learned my grandma's first husband, your father, died of TB, she became a bit more understanding about her mother's emotional distance."

Maybe Grandma had felt guilty bonding with her children after having left George in England to be raised by the Dalys.

George frowned. "So she wasn't a kind mother?"

"She was kind, just didn't share her past or some of her feelings with family. That hurt my mom and her sisters."

"How many sisters does she have?"

"Two, Dottie and Teri. They're all in their fifties."

"It may take them a bit to get over the shock. I've had eight years to process the news. I was quite upset that I wasn't told sooner, providing me the opportunity to meet Bridget Coffey, who I'd assumed had already passed away when I learned of her. My family didn't have contact with the Dalys in Ireland."

George listened with interest while I told him about his aunt Emily Ryan, who spent holidays at the Daly estate next to Grandma's childhood home. How she'd provided what little knowledge I had about Grandma's life in Ireland. How Grandma and John Michael had met.

"All my mother could tell me was that Bridget's family were tenant farmers on the Daly land and my parents marrying each other estranged them from family," he said. "They must have really been in love to fight all odds to be together. She thought she was giving me a chance at a better life and didn't want me torn between two feuding families. I would love to meet your mother. You must all come for a visit. The Dalys made their money off Irish tenant farmers like your grandmother's family. It's as much your estate as mine." His kind smile included his gray eyes. "After all, we're family."

Yes, we were.

"I can see the reasons behind her decisions and don't feel it's my place to judge her," he said.

That was generous and open-minded of him, since *I* was having a difficult time not judging Grandma. I felt bad over leaving behind a dog in Ireland I'd never even met. I couldn't imagine if Mr. MacCool were a child. If *I* felt this way, how would Mom respond to having a half brother kept from her? Grandma hadn't merely left her buried husband in England, but a child. What other secrets had she left behind when she'd immigrated to America?

❧ ❧

My mind was still reeling after two hours chatting with George about our families and life on the Daly estate in Lancashire. He gave me the photos. I wondered if Mom would stick his wedding photo in the drawer with his parents' pic or if she'd even want it. I'd put him in touch with Sadie Collentine, Grandma's niece in Killybog, Ireland, who lived just up the road from the Daly and Coffey homes. I requested that he allow me to contact his aunt Emily first to ease the shock. I hoped I could keep my promise about Mom being in touch soon. After all, she couldn't blame George for being her half brother, could she?

I whisked past the front of La Haute Bohème, not wanting my coworkers to see me if they were just heading back to their rooms. I felt bad having ditched them, but better them than George. I hid in a doorway around the corner and called Rachel. I'd phoned her and Declan earlier about capturing Oscar and saving my reputation, so I went right into George Wood's shocking news.

"Holy shit," she muttered.

"What are we going to do?"

"I have no clue."

Seriously? Rachel was always the one with a plan. The one who could think rationally under pressure. That was why I always asked myself, *What would Rachel do in this situation?*

"I mean, we have to tell Mom," I said. "We can't not tell her. Right?"

"Yeah, we have to tell her. Holy shit," she muttered again. "I just don't know *how* we're going to tell her. There's no chance he's lying, is there?"

"Why would he lie?"

"Maybe he thinks we're rich."

"He doesn't need money." I described the Daly estate in England and told her about George's offer for us to visit the home he believed was ours as much as his.

Rachel gasped. "What if he plans to leave it to our family in his will? If you hadn't connected with him, the house might have become a funeral home. Cool old houses are always turned into funeral homes."

"He didn't say he was leaving us the estate. It was a figure of speech. And I'm not researching our family history hoping to find some long-lost rich relative."

"No, but it could be a bonus."

Family was slowly becoming more important to Rachel than work, but some things about her might never change.

"Besides, I'm sure there's an heir to the estate, some third cousin," I said.

"Maybe that's no longer how it works. Or it's privately owned, not an *estate* per se."

"Can we please focus on a plan for telling Mom right now?"

"I can't focus. My head is ready to explode. Let's regroup and talk tomorrow morning."

I agreed.

I called Declan and got his voicemail. I left a message that George Wood had some interesting news and hadn't intended to abduct me. He texted that he'd call me soon. It was times like this I wanted to be able to hop into a car and drive over to my boyfriend's house to share the news, a hug, and moral support.

Despite the fact that I didn't own a car.

As much as I dreaded facing Blair, it would be easier to get it over with now than to wait until morning. And I'd feel bad going to my room if the staff was still working. I entered the office with a sense of dread to find Blair sitting alone at her desk. She gave me a peeved look, her maroon lips pursed, making her chin and cheekbones look even sharper.

"I'm sorry I wasn't able to come back to help."

"We got it done," she said in a clipped tone.

"I had a family emergency. I just met a half uncle I never knew existed."

While I recounted the story, she didn't even fake interest. No flicker of curiosity in her dark eyes. No look of compassion for the life-altering news I was still processing.

"It's hard when family matters come up on-site and you're far away from home," she said. "I've missed two uncles' funerals. It's just as hard making the choice in advance between work and personal obligations. I missed my sister's wedding two years ago. My mom didn't talk to me for six months. And I've missed my husband's birthday the last four years because of an annual meeting."

She hadn't missed a *beat* turning my shocking news into a discussion on the consequences of choosing personal obligations over professional ones.

"You don't regret any of the choices you made?" I asked.

Her gaze narrowed, surprised I was putting her on the spot. I wasn't doing it to be confrontational. Well, maybe a little. But after Rachel's comment about me making time to meet with George Wood or regretting it, I seriously wanted to know how Blair felt about her choices.

She shrugged. "I'd have regretted losing my job more. My husband has come to accept that traveling a hundred and fifty days a year is part of who I am."

Rachel was a full-time planner, but she traveled half that. She'd still missed plenty of family events.

"He'd be pissed if I lost my job. We used my frequent flyer miles for a Tahiti trip last year and Bali the year before."

What if her hubby decided he wanted a woman who would be there to share all their special occasions? Maybe he already had one. Blair spent every Valentine's Day with Mr. Gauthier. I didn't want Declan and me to ever accept the fact that we only saw each other a few days every month or two. However, Declan canceling our Chicago trip to book the Amsterdam meeting made me worried that he *did* accept it.

Blair's phone rang.

"Speak of the devil. My husband. I'll call him back later." She tossed her phone to the side. "Be down at five. I'm going to have you do departures. The ground company rep will be here around ten. I know you have to depart at noon." Another call rang on her phone. "It's the client. I have to take this."

She wasn't going to ask me to work the Monte Carlo incentive like she'd told Mindy. Now Declan and I wouldn't be able to meet up in April or May. After St. Paddy's Day, when were we going to see each other again?

Yet I felt a sense of relief rather than disappointment over not having to work with Blair again or be subjected to such a toxic work environment. I didn't get why the staff continued working for her. Money? With the instability of the job, they couldn't afford to turn one down, never knowing what was next. On that first Dublin meeting, one of the reasons I'd decided to continue with this job was the appeal of being my own boss and having control over whom I worked for and when.

But ultimately, the job controlled me, not vice versa.

After I'd hunted down the macaron thief, Blair knew my strong work ethic and determination, yet she was on the fence about my judgment. So on the Monte Carlo program I'd still have had to prove myself when the shit hit the fan, which it would because it always did. This was going to be the case with every new planner. And according to Mindy and Chad, I'd be taking on new clients for the rest of my career, or at least trying to.

Crap. I never responded to Declan's client about the Miami gig in April.

Had I subconsciously failed to do so?

CHAPTER
SEVENTEEN

I sat at my guest room desk, wrapped in my new spa robe doused in pillow spray, sipping Irish tea and munching on Taytos, composing an e-mail accepting the Miami meeting. My phone rang. Rachel. Excellent. She must have figured out a way for us to tell Mom about George.

"This chick is going to be the death of me." Rachel let out a frustrated growl. "She's a complete idiot, then uses me as the scapegoat. I'm going to fly to Dublin and smack her."

She was referring to Gemma, an admin assistant at Flanagan's beer. She was at a hotel working the small executive meeting that I'd helped Rachel plan. My only work in January.

"Forget the March and April meetings they want me to do. I don't have time to plan them, let alone rectify the mess this dimwit makes."

"I'm sure Matthew McHugh knows it's her fault. Precisely why he asks you to plan them."

"Well, I'm not doing any more Flanagan meetings unless I can have you go on-site. Like the one in April for fifty people. No way is she going to be able to handle it."

"I'd love to do it. What week is it?"

"Starts on the seventh."

Declan was working in Dublin until the eighth, so we could squeeze in a few days and see each other after all.

"I could also plan the March meeting and go on-site."

I knew Flanagan's CEO from my first meeting last fall. He'd been ecstatic at Christmas when I'd won the silent auction prize of cooking with Finn O'Brien and had my pic in the paper wearing Flanagan attire, unknowingly blocking the competitor logos behind us. I'd earned a bonus for helping get Brecker Dark into O'Brien's restaurants when I wasn't even a Brecker employee.

"The March one is only twenty people and not until the end of the month, after you're home from the Brecker trip. They wouldn't pay for your airfare back to Dublin." Rachel heaved an exasperated sigh. "Flanagan's needs a full-time planner."

"Or a competent admin assistant. When I was an assistant, I did a way better job than this woman." And I'd been fired from the job eight months ago. In my defense, Andy's stalking had made me a complete wreck. I hadn't been a stellar admin, but better than this Gemma woman. "*I* could do her job."

"You could. Actually...they might be open to hiring a full-time meeting contractor they don't have to give benefits."

A stable paycheck would be wonderful, but I needed health insurance, paid holidays, sick days... Travel was the only perk this job provided, and seeing the inside of hotels and airports rather than sightseeing attractions really wasn't a perk.

"You could work out of my office a few days a week, so I could give you some direction. But they aren't going to pay your air for the smaller programs."

"What if they didn't have to pay for it? That would be a huge cost savings." I almost had enough frequent flyer miles for an international ticket, and Declan had offered me some of the bazillion miles he'd banked up.

"Are you saying you'd pay your own airfare or that you want to work in Dublin?"

My heart raced. Work in Dublin? The thought of a stable job and living in Ireland about made me dizzy with excitement.

"Work in Dublin," I blurted.

Rachel let out a faint laugh. "Mom would kill me if you moved to Dublin. She still hasn't forgiven me for getting you into the industry, even though hiring you for that first meeting was her idea. She worries when you're gone for a *week*."

"She's doing much better. She no longer contacts me a half dozen times a day."

Silence filled the line.

"Are you serious?" Rachel asked.

"Yeah, I am."

"The cost of living in Dublin would be high compared to what the position would pay. Look at all the money you save living with Mom and Dad."

"But I'd have a full-time job and could get a roommate."

"Gee, who'd that be?"

My dog, Mr. MacCool. I hadn't been thinking Declan. Going from seeing each other every fifty days to shacking up would be crazy.

"Is Declan the reason you don't want me to move to Dublin?"

"No. It's just that picking up and moving to another country isn't that easy. Not like you're part of the EU. Who knows if you could even get a work visa."

"I can check into it. Why not at least propose it to your boss? I'm sure he'd rather have you focused on Brecker meetings. You'd spend a lot less time training me than you do troubleshooting all the crap this woman effs up."

No response.

What happened to all that faith Rachel supposedly had in me? Her apology on the phone the other day? Saying I'd come a long way since my first meeting in Dublin? Telling me not to allow Blair to shake my confidence? Had that been a bunch of lies to make me feel better?

"I know this would be a big step, but I really think I can handle it. I've worked every role on this meeting, even security, hunting down the macaron thief. And it's huge, two hundred attendees."

"But you've only gone on-site for five programs and been doing this job part time for a few months. You'd be in way over your head."

"I'm more qualified than the ditz doing it. And you had less experience when you started planning at

Brecker. You'd never been out of the country. Once I plan a few programs, I'll be good. These are cookie-cutter meetings. A room for twenty to fifty attendees, breaks, lunch, and an occasional reception or dinner. That's it."

"There is no such thing as a cookie-cutter meeting. For a reception, how many pieces of appetizers would you do per person? What would the meal guarantees be for a seventy-five-person meeting? What is room attrition in a contract?"

I scrambled for at least one answer.

"These are *basic* questions every planner should know. When you help me plan a meeting, I take care of all these details. I just have you make calls to check availability and maintain the registration. Executing a meeting and planning one are two very different jobs. This is crazy, Caity. You always do stuff on a whim, not thinking it through."

"I do not."

"How long have you been considering moving to Dublin?"

"Awhile."

"Five minutes isn't awhile. If you move there for Declan and you guys break up, you'll quit Flanagan's and move home."

"You still think I'm a quitter? And just because I let Andy screw up my last job, and my life temporarily, doesn't mean I'd let Declan. I don't want to be dependent on him. On any man."

"I just don't want you to make another mistake."

As if all I did was make mistakes.

"Let me run the contract planning past my boss, and

if he okays it, I'll talk to Matthew McHugh. Do that for a year so I can train you on actually *planning* a meeting."

"A *year*? That's crazy." *Stay calm. Don't go berserk because Rachel was hired as a planner with zero experience but thought I needed a year and a half to be qualified enough to get a job.* "How about a few *months*? After I help plan and go on-site for the March and April meetings?" That sounded reasonable.

"This is your only option right now, Caity. We'll talk later. I have to go fix this meeting."

Dead air.

Fuming, I put a death grip on my phone. Rachel thinking I was such a slow learner made me more furious than her calling me a quitter! Granted, I'd had a history of not sticking with stuff. I'd changed my major four times. I'd dropped French and my dream of studying in Paris after struggling through three language semesters. I'd never stuck with a boyfriend except for Andy for two long ignorant years. But I'd done the elf job three years in a row, and I'd graduated college. Even though Rachel was right, I'd be in over my head, I couldn't believe she wasn't even considering it.

This was my chance at a job where coworkers would know my work ethics, trust my judgment, and not wonder if I was a thief. I needed the stability that came with a steady paycheck, same boss, and same coworkers. To have a job that provided more balance between my personal and professional lives. Most of Flanagan's meetings were held in Dublin at their headquarters or the Connelly Court Hotel. I'd be home nights to eat dinner, walk Mr. MacCool, and meet friends for a pint. It'd been over two years since I'd done Martini Mondays with girlfriends.

Could the cost of living be that much higher in Dublin than Milwaukee? Despite Rachel being dead against me moving to Dublin and working for Flanagan's, I was curious and searched apartment rentals online. A tiny one-bedroom near St. Stephen's Green was almost $1,700 a month without utilities but with a lovely alley view. I'd have the added expense of internet, food...necessities my parents currently provided. Yet public transportation would eliminate the need for a car.

The dollar was currently tanking to the euro. I wouldn't have to worry about the exchange rate if I was paid in euros. And the job likely paid more in Dublin than back home due to the cost of living. An apartment in the north suburbs near Flanagan's headquarters would undoubtedly be cheaper than in the city center. And it would be close to the airport, so easy access for Declan flying in and out of town. Maybe he'd want to store stuff at my place since he'd be there when he was in town anyway. Right now he had belongings at his brother's in London and his parents'.

I stared at the Miami e-mail draft on my computer. My excitement faded, and an icky feeling tossed my stomach. Would the planner be a total nightmare like Blair? Would the meeting be more understaffed than this one? What if there were 1,500 attendees like one of Rita's meetings?

I started hyperventilating.

I frantically revised the e-mail, declining the meeting.

I hit Send.

Panic pressed against my chest.

What the hell had I just done? I needed work!

Was Rachel right? Was I a quitter?

My phone chimed. A text from Declan wondering if I could talk. I blew out a calming breath, attempting to get a grip before I called him. The downside of FaceTime was trying to hide your facial expressions.

Racks of wine bottles lined a stone wall behind Declan. "Just a sec. I'm going out of the cellar so I have better service." He passed by long wooden banquet tables lined with platters of food, wine bottles, flickering candles, and people loudly chatting. He headed up the stairs to a rustic room with flames dancing in a stone fireplace.

I told him about my visit with George Wood.

His eyes widened. "Jaysus. Didn't see that one coming, did ya? How are ya going to tell your mum?"

"No clue."

"Not sure how my mum would react to that."

"Not sure how mine will either."

"Maybe it'll get her to visit Ireland and England now and I can actually meet her."

I had to tell Mom about my relationship with Declan. Even if she wouldn't go to Ireland to visit, he'd be over to the States someday. Without Rachel's support, I certainly wouldn't be living in Ireland anytime soon.

I told Declan about my idea to plan Flanagan's meetings, leaving out that Rachel was against it.

"Brilliant. Get loads of experience helping Rachel so the CEO relies on you and can't imagine a meeting without ya. The Monte Carlo and Miami trips will look grand on your résumé."

"The Monte Carlo trip fell through and, ah, I turned down Miami."

Declan's gaze narrowed. "Why'd you turn it down?"

I'd panicked over possibly working another shit show like this one and had acted on impulse.

"To make myself go after the Flanagan's position," I lied.

I didn't want to admit I'd been irrational, deciding this job wasn't for me after only four months and a handful of meetings. I didn't want to sound like a quitter. He'd likely agree with Rachel that I hadn't given this job enough time. Were they right?

"What if you don't get it? Don't you think ya should have accepted the meeting until ya find out?"

Declan was usually my cheerleader. The one who had faith in my abilities when I didn't. Who helped me make light of my mishaps and reminded me I wasn't the only one who screwed up.

"You sound sure I wouldn't get the job. Do you think I'd be in over my head?"

"Well, you could use a wee more experience. The CEO is more likely to hire you as a contractor."

"What happened to *fake it till you make it*? You oversold me to Heather big time to get me on the Paris trip last fall."

"I was there to back you up."

Whoa. "You're not backing me up on this program, and I'm doing fine." Well, not *fine*, but I was surviving.

Declan shook his head with regret. "Sorry. Didn't mean it like that."

How else could he have meant it?

"You're telling me stories about mishaps all the time," I said. "What about you falling down bus stairs in front of a group? Why are mine any worse?" Because they happened more frequently and I handled them more poorly?

"They're not. I'm sorry." He started pacing away from the fireplace.

"If I lived in Dublin, we'd be able to see each other more."

"You wanna live *together*?" Declan came to an abrupt halt, his expression frozen, panic flickering in his eyes.

The benefit of FaceTime.

"That's not what I'm saying. Wouldn't you want me to move to Dublin? Do you like only seeing each other every fifty days?" Maybe Declan was booking a full schedule because he only wanted to hook up a day here and there. I refused to settle for a part-time relationship like Mindy and Blair each had.

"No, I'd like to see ya more. You're just throwing this all at me kind of fast." Declan slipped off his suit jacket.

It was likely our conversation, not the fireplace, making him sweat.

My hand was shaking so badly I could barely hold the phone steady, and I couldn't keep the trembling from my voice. "Again, we just went fifty days without seeing each other. Most couples at least live in the same country, for God's sake."

"I don't *live* in Ireland."

"You're there more than anywhere else. Besides, I wouldn't be moving there just for you, so don't freak out."

"Jaysus." He raked a frustrated hand through his hair.

"Sometimes I seem to be working harder at seeing each other than you are."

Declan's gaze sharpened. "What does that mean? I flew to Prague to see ya."

"That'd been my idea. So was meeting up in Chicago, and then you booked the Amsterdam trip without even telling me."

"I don't control how the programs fall. I wasn't hiding the trip from ya. It's on the calendar. I just forgot to mention it. I'm sorry. I should have said something."

"It's on the calendar because your flights linked to it. Why do you need to work twenty-seven days a month? That's insane. You work nonstop. You can afford to be more flexible than me."

Declan shifted his stance, glancing away.

Was it because he didn't want to see me?

"I hate not knowing if I might not see you for months." I shook my head in frustration. "This is way harder than I thought it would be."

Declan's eyes widened. "Saying ya wanna break up if ya don't move to Dublin?"

My head was spinning. "No, I don't know what I'm saying." This was crazy. We were arguing over me moving to Dublin and working at Flanagan's when I knew I couldn't do it without Rachel's blessing. "Let's talk later."

Click. Declan vanished.

That was the first time I'd ever hung up on him. If I hadn't, I feared I'd have said something I'd regret. I couldn't believe I'd just said everything I had after all the sweet things Declan had done for me this past week. But it'd been bugging me that he'd booked the Amsterdam trip, despite our plans for Chicago, without telling me, ruining my opportunity to do a big birthday surprise for him.

And like Rachel, he thought I couldn't handle this job without him. Maybe they were right. I had to stop calling them for advice when things went to hell. But I was also calling my boyfriend and sister, not merely a coworker and client. More so than the job, I couldn't believe Declan thought we were moving too fast and seemed satisfied with the way things were.

Was Rachel right—my main reason for wanting to move to Dublin was to live with Declan? And now Declan didn't even want me living in Dublin?

I collapsed onto the chair. I e-mailed the planner for the Miami meeting, claiming I'd misread my schedule and was available. How depressing that this job might provide my only stability at the moment.

I felt like I was losing everything I'd worked so hard for the past six months. Declan, my job, my relationship with Rachel, and what little financial stability I had gained were all biting the dust.

CHAPTER
EIGHTEEN

My 4:00 a.m. wake-up call was a text alert from Mom, wondering about my visit with George Wood. If I was still coming to terms with Grandma having a son, I couldn't deal with Mom's reaction in my current mindset and lack of caffeine.

On the way to the lobby to work departures, I opened an e-mail from Zoe with a pic of Mr. MacCool and her in matching green velvet leprechaun hats and tutus with gold sparkly shamrocks.

Thought maybe you and Mr. MacCool could wear these in the Dublin St. Paddy's Day parade. No worries. You don't have to be reserved to walk in the bloody thing. People crash it all the time. My girlies and I'll crash it with ya.

I'd be working a Brecker meeting rather than crashing the parade. However, I smiled at the thought of Zoe and her friends coming to Dublin for the holiday and a girls' night out.

Except for a front desk clerk, Mindy was alone in the

lobby, sitting on a red velvet chair, sipping a cup of coffee. It didn't take two of us to see off an early VIP departure. Blair was punishing me. Mindy spotted me and popped up from the chair, looking perky in her wrinkle-free suit, shiny pink earrings, and a pink silk scarf tied around her neck. I looked like I'd slept in my clothes, even though I'd barely slept.

"Sorry I wasn't there to help with the emergency last night." I gave Mindy an abbreviated version of my visit with George Wood while I made a cup of complimentary tea from a hot beverage display on a marble-topped table.

Her jaw dropped, and she placed a hand on my arm. "Wow, I don't blame you for not showing up. I wish I hadn't. It was a false alarm."

Yet Blair had made me feel guilty for not having been there?

"Blair thought a speaker was going to need a print job done for a meeting he's headed to today. I ended up rushing back from the castle for nothing. At least I made it as far as the courtyard this time."

How many meetings would I have to work in Prague to finally have a chance to visit the castle?

After Mindy stuck the VIP in a sedan, we went to the hotel coffee shop just off the lobby. Glass cases displayed an assortment of pastries and breads. We both ordered an apple strudel. Mindy opted for a double espresso, while I took the plunge and ordered a black coffee, which I never drank. I needed the caffeine for my long, depressing trip home. We sat at a small round mosaic-topped table. Steam rose to my face, and I inhaled the scent of fresh roasted coffee. I was about to take my first sip when Chad strolled in dressed in blue sweatpants and a white T-shirt and tennies. Must be nice to have the time and energy to work out at five in the morning.

He removed an earbud from his ear. "Guess I'm going to see you in Monte Carlo," he told Mindy. "Didn't have a schedule conflict after all. Asked Blair about it last night, and she still needed one staff."

Blair would obviously rather hire this lazy loser than me. I now sympathized with Gretchen, understanding her bitterness toward incompetent people stealing her work. Gretchen could be nasty, but she knew her stuff and was dependable.

"Awesome," Mindy said. "I'm going to extend a day so I can take the train over to Portofino and stare out at the Mediterranean all day, drinking Chianti."

Chad let out an exaggerated sigh, like he was so busy. "I have to head to DC the day it ends."

Mindy peered over at me. "You should extend with me. That'd be a blast."

I nodded faintly.

Chad left with a large coffee and grin.

"Blair didn't ask me to work the Monte Carlo meeting," I confessed.

Mindy's gaze narrowed. "Maybe she just hasn't gotten around to it."

I doubted that.

"I'm working a meeting in Chicago in June. The planner is looking for a few local staff. I'll recommend you."

Even after finding me in a suite wearing the VIP's slippers, Mindy was willing to hire me, unlike Blair.

I managed a smile, not wanting to appear unappreciative. "Thanks." I glanced toward the lobby. "I should see if the driver is here yet for Courtney and Rita's departure."

"Oh, they were hopping into a taxi when I got down at four. Courtney changed to an earlier flight. Cost almost a grand, but she didn't give a rip."

"I wouldn't either if I were her."

"Exactly."

Mindy had to pack, so we said our good-byes, hugging, promising to stay in touch, even though she didn't do social media. I mentally added her to my Christmas card list like so many other people I'd met over the past few months that I knew I might only communicate with once a year, like Madame Laurent and her dog, Esmé, in Paris.

I stood in the lobby, reviewing the departure manifest on my clipboard. Ted had departed the hotel at 3:00 a.m. I slipped my name badge from the plastic holder and tore it up. A dog barked. Startled, I dropped the shreds of paper, which scattered like confetti on the tiled floor.

Madam Petrov and Fritzie were bundled up for their morning walk. She had on her purple coat and matching wool hat. Fritzie wore a purple sweater. The dog growled, his beady brown eyes glaring at me. With a determined walk, the woman detoured toward the other side of the lobby.

"Excuse me," I called out, following them.

She came to an abrupt halt, staring at me with an intimidating gaze.

I cleared my throat. "Do you speak English?"

Her look turned wary. "Small bit."

I took an encouraging breath. "Are you related to the Petrov vodka family?"

She shook a finger at me, spatting a few harsh words in Russian, looking seriously offended, as if I were soliciting her for donations to my worthy cause.

"To Sasha Petrov?" I said. "Are you her sister, Natalya?"

She snapped her mouth shut and slowly lowered her finger, wearing a curious expression.

If she came here often, it seemed like she must believe the spirit of her sister was still alive in the hotel. That she was hoping for a connection. People came into our lives for a reason. Maybe my purpose and Mr. Gauthier's was to provide this woman with a bit of comfort. She didn't appear to be a very happy person.

"The nice man in the elevator who gave you his hanky was staying in the Bridal Suite." I pointed at the elevator and pretended to blow my nose, as if all the sign language might help her understand.

She looked confused.

Fritzie let out a bark.

"Is everything all right here?" the concierge asked, materializing. He conversed with Madam Petrov in Russian, then turned to me. "She is unsure what you are asking her."

"Tell her that Mr. Gauthier, the nice man in the elevator who gave her his hanky to wipe up Fritzie's pee, was staying in the Bridal Suite."

"Why should she care about such a thing?"

"Why would she keep coming to the hotel where her sister died? She's hoping for a connection."

The man's top lip curled back with disgust. "A dog's urine on a hanky is a connection?"

"People will grasp at anything." Grandma's picture on my nightstand gave me comfort, like she was watching over me. "And Fritzie really connected with Mr. Gauthier. It's a sign. I know it is. Can you please just tell her."

The concierge once again looked at me like I was nuts, but reluctantly translated my message.

The woman's features softened. She removed the hanky from her coat pocket. Eeww. However, it was no longer pee stained and appeared to have been washed, ironed, and folded with care. Something had possessed her to keep it. She massaged the soft material between her fingers, then slipped it back into her pocket. She gave me an appreciative smile, deep crinkles appearing around her gray eyes.

Madam Petrov and Fritzie headed toward the door, and I smiled at the bounce now in both of their steps. I turned to the concierge, who looked a bit baffled. "Thank you."

He arched a brow. "You're a peculiar woman, Ms. Shaw. Kind, but peculiar. It's been interesting."

"Better than being boring." Usually.

He smiled faintly. "Indeed." He turned and walked off.

When the ground company rep arrived midmorning and relieved me of my duties, I headed down to the office to tell Blair good-bye and good riddance. Before entering the room, I received a text from Declan.

Sorry. Can we talk?

I about collapsed with relief that we were still speaking.

Going into a meeting, then to airport. Will call at airport. Took Miami job.

I love you. He attached a pic of a cartoon sheep blowing a kiss.

I smiled. *Love you too.*

I was relieved we were still speaking, even though I was hurt that Declan had freaked out over the mere thought of us living together and that he didn't believe I could handle this job without him having my back. Even though he'd talked me into finding the cricket and off the ledge over the missing macarons... That was stuff a boyfriend would do.

Gretchen was alone in the office. I almost didn't recognize her without the jade eyeshadow and thick black liner. Her eyes didn't look as green, or as wicked. Her black suit jacket hung on the back of the chair, and her hair was pulled up in a loose twist. Was her casual appearance because it was the last day, or she was saying screw it?

"Blair's at the hotel post-con," she said. "I'm doing one later with Nigel since I don't leave until tomorrow. But here's his gratuity." She handed me a white envelope. "I thought you might want to give it to him. He'd mentioned visiting the States next month, so I gave him dollars."

That was considerate. Both the dollars and that Gretchen had listened to Nigel's vacation plans.

"Ah, thanks. That'd be great."

"He certainly has an interesting family history."

"Yeah, you just never know."

A look of longing filled her eyes. "No, sometimes you'll never know."

"If you want, I could do some research for you."

Had I seriously just said that? What about wanting to start my Flannery research? It was the money talking. Yet I could sympathize with Gretchen wondering about her family history after losing her father at a young age. Omigod. That was the second time this morning that I'd sympathized with her.

Gretchen gave me an appreciative smile. Her most sincere one ever. "That'd be great."

I killed the awkward bonding moment by talking pay. "I usually charge a $250 flat rate, if that's okay." I wasn't prepared to request as much as Nigel had offered to pay, but I could slowly raise my rate as I became more competent.

"Sounds good." She pulled two hundred dollars from her wallet. "Would it be okay if I paid the rest in euros?"

She could pay the rest in yen or pesos for all I cared.

My first cash client.

"Sure."

She counted out the remaining payment. "I'll send you what little info I have. I think my grandpa came from Germany."

Germany. That was a new one.

"I've always dreamed of retiring in a little mountain village in Bavaria. Too bad it was my grandpa born there and not my dad, or I'd get dual citizenship."

"Yeah, I'd love to have Irish citizenship."

"Why don't you get it? You're eligible since your grandma was born there. Citizenship requirements vary by country. My friend's grandpa was from Ireland, and she got dual citizenship."

Seriously? I was going to look into that, pronto. Excitement zipped through me at the prospect of traveling with an Irish passport. It would be a step in the right direction. To one day live in Ireland.

Blair walked in, and tension filled the air. There'd been more friction between Blair and Gretchen than Blair and me over the macaron theft. They'd barely spoken since Gretchen had called her out about being as guilty as anyone for stashing stuff under tables.

"I'm going to grab a coffee," Gretchen said, not offering to get Blair one.

"I'll be in touch," I told her.

Something I never imagined saying to Gretchen.

She smiled her thanks and walked out.

"Do you have a sec?" Blair's tone was much pleasanter than last night.

What was up?

I sat down at her desk.

"I was cc'd on an e-mail Mr. Gauthier sent to the client this morning. He thought the meeting went well and had a lot of praise for the staff. He requested you for their Monte Carlo trip in May." She smiled despite her tightened jaw. "Hopefully, you're available."

It had to be killing her that her "boyfriend" was requesting me, forcing her to put me on that meeting. Especially after she'd just hired Chad for the last position.

"So I'd be on VIPs with Mindy?"

"I only need one staff for the role. I'll give Mindy a break. Put her on something else."

Supposedly *this* meeting had only required one staff for VIPs. Flying solo when it came to accommodating VIPs' needs would be major stress. Yet I couldn't believe I'd impressed Mr. Gauthier enough by attempting French and risking life and limb to get him his key that he'd requested me on the next program. A sense of pride consumed me.

"Can you check your calendar?" Blair asked.

"Sure. I'll get back to you."

I wanted to get back to Blair that I wasn't available. But I had to stick with this job until I found something else. At least making her wait for my response gave me a semblance of control. Maybe my *Póg Mo Thóin*—Kiss My Ass—undies I was wearing were giving me a false sense of bravado. Maybe the reason Blair had come into my life was to give me a push in the right direction. To show me that meetings weren't all like the ones I'd worked for Rachel and Heather with small groups, sane planners, and time to sightsee.

I found Nigel in the main ballroom, setting for an event that evening with the Grateful Dead guy's band. The elegant room had been transformed into Haute Goth done in black, gold, and iron décor. I told him about my discovery with George Wood.

"You just never know what skeletons you might uncover in your research."

I hoped I didn't find anything too bad lurking in Nigel's family's past. I handed him his gratuity envelope, thanking him.

He handed it back. "You keep it as a down payment on my research. You can let me know any outstanding amount."

"What if it's too much?"

"Learning my family history is priceless." He winked. He handed me a cardboard box with a small package of French macarons resting on top. "The sugar bowl and creamer set. And I threw in a cake plate to serve the macarons."

I smiled at his dry sense of humor. It'd be nice to stay in touch with the kind banquet manager and have communication with the outside world when I was hibernating in my bedroom, snowbound in Milwaukee.

"I thought Gretchen might prefer some Bohemian wine flutes and a bottle of Prosecco," he said.

"Perfect. I think she'll need a drink tonight."

I went to shake Nigel's hand, but he placed a hand on my arm, a kiss to my cheek. "Safe travels home."

I walked down the hallway, discreetly tearing open the envelope. Four hundred bucks! Along with Gretchen's payment, I couldn't remember the last time I'd had so much cash on me. At least not cash that was *mine* rather than company petty cash for VIP shopping. I wondered if that was a typical tip or if Gretchen had been overly generous. Not a word I ever dreamed I'd use to describe Gretchen.

Did Gretchen now use different words to describe me also?

CHAPTER NINETEEN

I was in my room packing when I received an e-mail from Mom checking again on George and forwarding the link to a new fish fry place we were going to Friday, Earl and Francine's Supper Club. Their garlic mashed potatoes were supposedly to die for. Artery-clogging potatoes. That was what I had to look forward to. Not a very Irish attitude, but I'd rather be sitting in a Dublin pub eating mashed potatoes off the top of a shepherd's pie.

I couldn't put off calling Mom any longer. I'd tell her that George Wood's story was long and better shared when I got home. This wasn't the type of information I should hit her with over the phone, especially if she was alone at the time. Grandma's secret first marriage would pale in comparison to Mom's secret half brother.

Mom answered on the second ring. "I didn't think you were going to ever call me."

"Sorry. I met with George Wood late last night, and I had to be up at four this morning."

"That's not what I'm referring to. However, I do want to hear about your visit. I'm referring to the fact that you want to work in Dublin."

I couldn't believe Rachel had told Mom about my interest in moving to Dublin. I felt like I was ten years old.

"Ah, yeah, sorry. I didn't think Rachel would nark on me. Besides, I decided against it."

"Did you and Declan break up?" Her voice filled with concern.

"What did Rachel tell you about us?"

"She didn't have to tell me anything. I'm not blind. Your face lights up every time you mention him. You're all happy after he calls. And yes, I know he calls. I've been a mother for almost thirty years."

"I'm sorry I didn't tell you about us sooner, but I didn't want you to think I was making another mistake." Like Rachel had. "And no, we didn't break up."

"Because you had one bad relationship I'm going to think you'll have another? Mistakes are how we learn. One of my big regrets was not taking a summer job at my aunt's clothing boutique in Napa Valley. I chose to stay in Wisconsin and work at Camp Burning Nettles instead to be close to your father. Of course that wasn't the actual name of the camp, but almost everyone got burning nettles that summer, including me, and it made all the counselors' jobs a complete nightmare..."

While Mom described how to identify the nasty plant when out hiking in the woods—which I did, never—I tried to process exactly where this conversation was headed.

"Anyway," she said, coming up for air. "I'm surprised you aren't going to give this job opportunity a shot."

Rachel and Declan thought I was nuts for even considering moving to Dublin, whereas *Mom* thought I should go for it? Or was this reverse psychology?

"So you're telling me to go for the job?"

"Of course I don't *want* you to move to Ireland, but luckily your aunt Dottie was here when Rachel called. She convinced me to take the night to calm down and think about this before talking to you." Mom let out a deep sigh of resignation. "She also reminded me of my regret over not having done the summer in Napa. I don't want you to live with the regret of not doing this. Don't get me wrong—I love your father and don't regret marrying him, most of the time. But I should have taken that summer for myself. And I was only nineteen. You're almost twenty-five. I'll worry about you no matter what age you are—that's what mothers do. But you did fine on your own at Christmas, and you have people in Ireland who care about you."

In shock, I was unable to utter a word.

"I hope you're still there after I just rambled on forever," she said.

"Yeah, ah, I'm still here. This Dublin job wouldn't just be temporary, like for a summer." Despite what Rachel believed.

"I realize that."

I could picture Mom nodding, trying to maintain a calm and rational tone despite her reservations. Like the time she'd walked into my bedroom and found me painting it neon orange and black, our school colors.

"Dublin is only a seven-hour flight. It's about time I visited Ireland. Breakfast is almost ready..." She had a brief side conversation with my dad. "Your father's up.

Why don't we discuss George Wood's family history when you get home?"

"Ah, sounds good. Love you."

Rachel and Declan might not think I could handle this job, but Mom and Mr. Gauthier did? Rachel was going to flip if she found out Mom had sided with me rather than her, something that rarely happened. And Mom was right about regrets. Wasting two years with Andy was my biggest one yet, but losing Declan would be an even bigger one if our long-distance relationship failed.

Flanagan's meetings wouldn't be nearly the stress of this job. Much of my current stress came from constant jet lag, sleeping in unfamiliar beds, and having no routine or balance. Like I'd told Rachel, Flanagan's meetings were small, cookie-cutter meetings. Granted, I wasn't familiar with negotiating hotel contracts or planning meal guarantees, but most of the off-site meetings were at the Connelly Court Hotel, so they likely had standard provisions. I could take an online Meeting Planning 101 class and learn the basics within a few months, despite Rachel thinking it'd take me *years*.

Rachel was still never going to go for it.

What if I pitched the idea directly to Flanagan's CEO?

My taking initiative might impress him. And I'd paved the way for Brecker landing Finn O'Brien's business. Telling the CEO I'd applied for dual citizenship would make me look serious about moving to Ireland. That this wasn't some spur-of-the-moment whim like Rachel feared. If the pay wasn't great, I'd pick up a part-time job. Maybe Gerry Coffey needed help at the pub.

The thought of going back to snow, four thousand miles from Declan and Ireland, about made me burst into tears. Financial stability meant nothing without emotional stability. I was always asking myself what Rachel would do in a situation.

Rachel would go after this job.

My life had looked bleak until my first trip to Ireland and meeting Declan, both of which made me feel grounded. Suddenly, I didn't want to waste another second. Rachel had cc'd me on an e-mail with Flanagan's CEO while planning the current Dublin meeting, so I had his addy. I shot off an e-mail telling him I was in Dublin for a few days and asked if he'd have time to meet.

My palms started sweating, my heart racing. I couldn't believe I'd just gone behind Rachel's back. I'd been working so hard at rebuilding our relationship. My ancestry research had helped us reconnect and had brought us closer together and closer to Mom. We'd become friends, not just sisters. However, Rachel more than anyone should understand this was a professional decision, not a personal one. And she'd told me not to be a quitter, so I was going for this job.

Besides likely having alienated my sister, what if I couldn't change my airline ticket or get a decent-priced hotel room in Dublin? I e-mailed our sales rep at the Connelly Court Hotel to see if she'd give me a deal on a room. If not, I'd stay at the River Liffey dump. I checked my airline reservation. A change to my current return ticket of Prague to Chicago would cost $600 with fees and availability. Luckily, if I flew Aer Lingus instead, a new one-way ticket for Dublin to Chicago was only $250, and a ticket from Prague to Dublin was $100. The cash from Nigel and Gretchen would cover my trip.

Within a half hour, the CEO confirmed he could meet tomorrow at 2:00 p.m.

I did a mental happy dance. Then my stomach dropped.

He'd cc'd Rachel on the e-mail.

He likely assumed our appointment was about their upcoming meetings since I'd helped Rachel plan the one currently taking place. Rachel was going to go ballistic. She hated being blindsided. I had to call her before she read the e-mail. I set the alarm on my phone for 6:05 a.m. Milwaukee time.

Hopefully, she was still talking to me.

❧❦ ❦❧

I stood in line at the Aer Lingus ticket counter, immersed in the sound of Irish accents and tourist attractions displayed on overhead monitors: Birr Castle, Cliffs of Moher, Ring of Kerry...

My phone alarm chimed, and my stomach clenched.

Time to call Rachel.

She answered on the first ring. "I can't believe you went behind my back like that."

She'd obviously read her e-mail.

"I'm sorry. But I was down to the wire. I'm leaving Prague today. It's ideal timing for me to stop in Dublin."

"You should have at least told me before contacting him. *I* got you the work with Flanagan's. They're part of *my* company."

"Mom forced you to put me on that first meeting. If I hadn't proved I could do the job, you wouldn't have hired me for those other meetings or had me helping you plan Flanagan's." A group of girls ahead of me were shooting curious glances my way. I lowered my voice. "You'd have expected me to understand that it was a professional decision, not a personal one."

"Well, this feels personal. And me not wanting you to take the job was also personal. I worry about you, Caity. You're still recovering from your relationship with Andy. I don't think it's smart to make such a major move that at least partially revolves around a guy."

"I knew you'd have talked me out of it."

"Of course I would have. What if Matthew McHugh gets pissed, thinking I should have run it by him first before you put him on the spot? What if he thinks *I'm* putting him on the spot? You've put me in a really shitty position. If they hire a planner for the first time, they're going to want someone who can hit the ground running."

"I'm more competent than Gemma, even if you don't think so."

"What is that supposed to mean?"

"You think it'd take me a year and a half to be qualified for a planner position when you got one with no experience. I've worked Matthew McHugh's meetings. He knows I'm more capable than Gemma. And I'm not in *way* over my head." Just a bit. "I'm going to sign up for an online meeting planning class, and I'm looking into applying for Irish dual citizenship. If I don't move there for a job at Flanagan's, I'm moving there for another one."

"I just can't believe you did this without telling me."

Her hurt and disappointed tone caused my confidence to waver.

"You know why I sent that e-mail?" I wasn't going to say *Mom* and put her in the middle of this. Besides, Mom and Rachel had both played a role in my decision.

"Hmph?"

"I always ask myself, 'What would Rachel do in this situation?' And in this situation, I knew you'd go for the job."

"Seriously?" Rachel sounded like she'd had the wind knocked out of her. "You think I'd have gone behind your back like that? I wouldn't have. Not now. Not knowing what it could do to our relationship. Maybe the old Rachel would have done that, but the old *Caity* never would have."

Click.

Wow. Low blow. I'd always admired my sister's ambition and determination, but I'd vowed not to turn out like her, allowing my job to control my life and putting it before family and friends.

Had I just done that?

I was torn whether I believed that Rachel wouldn't have done the same thing in my shoes. I didn't blame her for being ticked that I hadn't given her a heads-up that I was sending the e-mail. Yet if I had, I wouldn't have gone through with it. And I felt this was something I really needed to do. I would pitch the job in a way that wouldn't reflect badly on Rachel. I'd mention that I was moving to Dublin and currently looking for a planner's position. I didn't have to admit Flanagan's was the only place I was looking. If the CEO didn't bite, I'd mention the contract planning idea. Yet I couldn't afford to live in Dublin and contract plan without benefits. As a contract planner, I'd need to still live at home and for Rachel to allow me in her office.

I called Declan, but he didn't answer. Since this wasn't something I should leave in a voicemail, I said I'd try him later. I didn't want to tell him I was going to Dublin until I knew how the interview went.

An American couple standing behind me were chatting about their first trip to Ireland. "There's no way Ireland will be as beautiful as Prague," the man said.

"It'll be hard to beat," his wife replied.

I turned toward the middle-aged couple. "Prague is beautiful, but Ireland is breathtaking. All the shades of green are like a patchwork quilt, even in winter. The grass is the most cushiony carpet ever. Ivy wraps around huge tree trunks, and thick hedges divide fields. Sheep are everywhere." I laughed at the thought of Zoe and me herding the red and green dyed sheep off the road. "The countryside is so peaceful, you can hear sheep baaing and cows mooing five fields away. The people are the nicest ever. They welcome you into their homes like they've known you all their lives." I smiled, consumed by an overwhelming sense of longing to visit Declan's parents in the country.

"Do you work for the Irish tourism board?" the man joked, jarring me from my mental tour of Ireland.

"No, but I'll add that to my list of possible jobs. Thanks."

"Do you live there?" the woman asked. "Heading home?"

I smiled, nodding, a warm feeling rushing through me.

Declan was a wonderful reason to move to Ireland, but he definitely wasn't my only one. I had plenty of others. Zoe, Sadie Collentine and her cousin Seamus Quinn, Declan's parents, Mr. MacCool, Nicholas Turney...George Wood. I could hop over to England for a weekend at the Daly estate and learn how to play cricket or ride a horse. Ireland gave me a sense of belonging and comfort no place ever had.

CHAPTER
TWENTY

I inhaled a deep breath, and the Connelly Court Hotel's signature vanilla-lavender scent filled my head. After tripping here in front of Brecker's CEO, along with other embarrassing mishaps, I never imagined this place would have such a calming effect on me. I crossed the white marble lobby, passing by a crystal vase filled with red and white roses from Valentine's Day. A very modern-feeling hotel compared to La Haute Bohème, except for the black-and-white 1930s and '40s Dublin photos on the walls. I pictured Grandma and her sister Theresa shopping at the large Roches department store for the dresses they'd worn in my picture, and John Michael twirling Grandma around the floor at the ballroom dance hall.

"Well, hello Ms. Shaw," a man said.

I turned from the photo to find the hotel's general manager. An older gentleman dressed in a black suit with a gray shirt and red tie. The last time we'd seen each other was right after I'd dragged a drunk attendee out from under the hotel's Christmas tree. The loser had his arm draped around my shoulder for support, giving the manager the impression we were a couple.

"So nice to have you back."

"It's wonderful to be back."

His gaze narrowed. "Not here with a group, are you?"

"No, just me this time."

How weird, being here without fifty attendees. Not having to avoid the lobby for fear of being bombarded with questions. Not waking up at the crack of dawn to work breakfast and open the hospitality desk. I could sleep in and order room service. Except I couldn't afford room service, even with the discounted rate the hotel's sales rep had given me.

"Ah, that's grand. Have a lovely stay."

"Thanks. I'm sure I will."

Fingers crossed the entire trip would be lovely.

Being here felt so right, yet my nerves were a wreck. What if I made a complete fool of myself in the meeting with the CEO? What if he wasn't even interested in plan B—hiring me as a contract planner in Milwaukee? Then I had to go to plan C—continue on-site contract work while looking for a full-time planner or coordinator job in Milwaukee. Yet even embellished, my résumé wasn't impressive. I had an "in" at Flanagan's, and I'd landed the contract jobs thanks to Declan's referrals.

I sucked in a lungful of the vanilla-lavender scent and headed up to my guest room to stash my luggage. I stuck the key into the slot inside the door, and the lights clicked on. A red throw was draped across the bed's white duvet. Black-and-white vintage photos of

Dublin hung on the walls. I remembered the night Declan and I had done ancestry research in his room and had almost shared our first kiss. He'd given me his hotel toiletries for Martha's women's shelter. A small yet compassionate gesture. That was the moment I'd really started falling for Declan.

He still hadn't returned my call. He likely assumed I was in the air over the Atlantic right now and unavailable.

I removed the Charles Bridge prints from my suitcase, making sure they hadn't been damaged during the flight. They hadn't fit in my carry-on bag with Declan's sketch. I arranged all three on the desk, with the sketch in the middle. Should I tell Declan the prints were hot? He'd probably get a kick out of the story. Now he'd have the prints, and I'd have the sketch, to remember that pivotal moment in our relationship when he'd drawn my picture.

I headed down to the lobby. I stepped outside and instinctively took a right down the sidewalk. I felt confident I wouldn't need a map, unlike the time I'd escorted Brecker's CEO's wife to a sweater shop and feared we'd wander into a sketchy neighborhood.

The scent of fish and chips drifted out from a takeaway place, and a lively Celtic tune poured out of a souvenir shop, along with two giggling girls in leprechaun hats and green boas. They reminded me of Zoe and me. Shops were already preparing for the onslaught of St. Paddy's Day visitors. I'd stop on my way back for a Flannery pin and green boa and garter I could wear for the holiday celebration, and for Declan. I wasn't sure how sexy he'd find the tutu Zoe had made me.

My first stop would be Coffey's pub to see if Gerry had a part-time job available in case the Flanagan's position didn't pay enough to support myself. I could learn to pull a pint or be a cocktail waitress. Rachel couldn't get upset at me for asking Gerry for a job when she'd claimed they were merely friends. My sister taking the initiative to find a pub with our Coffey surname had been a step toward us reconnecting. I feared I'd set our relationship back several years. But I'd make it right again.

I crossed a bridge over the Liffey, then headed down a side street away from the river. I encountered the green pub with gold lettering reading *Coffey's*. My mouth watered for Taytos. I'd eaten all but three bags of Declan's gift. Not in a touristy area, locals were stopping by after work for a pint. Soccer, rugby, and hurling team photos and memorabilia filled the walls.

Gerry Coffey was behind the long wooden bar, serving pints of Guinness. He was fortyish—ten years older than Rachel—dark hair, blue eyes, and a five o'clock shadow. His brown Jameson T-shirt showed off his biceps. He wiped frothy beer foam from the side of a glass and cleaned his hand on his jeans. Not Rachel's usual clean-cut businessman. She'd flirted the shirt off his back—a green *Coffey's Dublin* T-shirt—since they'd had none for sale. Rachel had in turn given it to me. I smiled at the souvenir T-shirts now for sale behind the bar.

Gerry spotted me, his eyes widening in surprise. "Well, if it isn't Miss Caity Shaw." He peered past me with a hopeful look.

"She's not with me. Sorry."

He smiled despite the disappointed glint in his eyes. "Jaysus, don't be apologizing. It's grand seeing ya."

I reached over the bar to shake his hand, and he drew me in, placing a kiss to each of my cheeks. "What brings ya to Dublin?"

I spilled my guts about my arguments with Declan and Rachel. He had the right to know my sister might be ticked if he gave me a job. I didn't want to cause a rift between them.

"Normally, I'd listen to her," I said. "I value her opinion and that she gave me this job, but this is something I have to do. I feel like if I don't do it, I'll regret it my entire life. You know what I mean?"

"Aye, I do indeed." He smiled, a reminiscent look on his face while he took a brief journey to Rachel-land. "The heart wants what the heart wants. Even if it gets broken."

If Rachel wasn't going to throw this guy a bone, I was. "She really likes you. She just sucks at showing her feelings." She was going to kill me, especially since I got upset when she stuck her nose in my relationship with Declan. I hadn't done well in emotional situations either, until Declan. My learning about Shauna's death had helped us both open up. "If I move here, she'll come to visit." I smiled, wanting to give us both hope. "Even if I do get the job, I'll likely need a part-time one. You wouldn't have one available, would you?"

He shook his head. "Sorry, luv. Nothing right now, but ya never know. How about your first lesson on how to pull a proper pint of Guinness so you'll be prepared if a position comes up?"

I smiled, stepping behind the bar with him. I grabbed a glass from the lower counter.

"Jaysus, don't be pouring a Guinness in that." A guy in a blue rugby shirt gestured to the competitor glass in my hand.

I exchanged it for a Guinness glass.

Gerry gave me a wink.

I held the glass under the Guinness tap.

"Gold harp to the back," the rugby guy said.

I turned the glass around so the gold Celtic harp emblem was facing away from me.

"At a forty-five-degree angle," his buddy added.

I eyed the guys. "Drank a few Guinness, have you?"

Gerry laughed. "Fair play to ya. You could handle the lads here."

My gaze glued to the gold harp, I pulled the tap toward me. A hissing noise filled the air as the beer filled the glass. Gerry straightened the glass in my hand as I slowly eased up on the tap until the beer reached the gold harp. I set the glass on the bar. The beer settled, turning darker, a thick foam forming on the top.

"Nitrogen is rising and the CO_2 is dropping, creating the foam. Now push back to finish filling. No nitrogen is released."

"Wow, I never knew Guinness was so high tech." I finished filling the glass.

"Now, ya do a taste test," the rugby guy said, holding up his pint.

I clinked his glass. "*Sláinte.*"

Gerry poured a pint and raised his glass. "Here's to your new job."

I wasn't sure if he was referring to Flanagan's or that he saw a bartending job in my near future, so I drank to both.

I entered the Connelly Court Hotel, still warm from two pints of Guinness. I needed to practice my pitch and get a good night's sleep so I was perky for my appointment. I'd already set my phone's alarm, afraid I'd sleep for two days straight, I was so exhausted. I strolled through the lobby, taking in the vintage photos, calming scent, and...Declan, seated in a red corner chair.

As if sensing my presence, he raised his gaze to mine, slowly standing. He held my gaze as he approached, a glint of caution in his blue eyes. My heart raced. My body grew even warmer. Only a few days since I'd seen him, but it felt like forever. He stopped just in front of me, and I opened my mouth to apologize but kissed him instead. I slipped my arms around his neck, and he slid his around my waist, drawing me against him.

When the kiss became too steamy for a public lobby, I reluctantly drew back. "Rachel?" I said. That was the only way he could have known I was there. Had she called and asked him to talk me out of it?

He nodded. "We thought you might be needing some moral support."

"Is there a difference between her support and her approval?"

He shrugged. "She's trying."

I smiled. "I was afraid she'd never speak to me again." However, this didn't mean she was *speaking* to me.

"She's not particularly happy *how* ya went about it, but she's accepting the fact ya did it. You'll be grand, make her proud."

I hoped so. "I'm sorry I didn't tell you I was coming here, but I didn't want to leave it in a voicemail. Your meeting isn't over, is it?"

"I left due to a family crisis."

My heart did a little tap dance at Declan referring to me as *family*.

"Must be nice. The only way Blair would have let me leave the meeting early would have been on a stretcher or in a straitjacket."

He gave me a sly grin. "They'll want me back. It's an American group, and they think my accent is cute."

That undoubtedly wasn't all they thought was cute.

"I'm sorry for wiggin' out on the phone," I said.

He slipped his arms from my waist, capturing my hand in his. "I have to admit I was a wee bit surprised when ya mentioned moving to Ireland. I wanna see ya more. I just wasn't prepared for ya to be living here so soon. One day, I'd hoped...but I'd love it to be now." He brushed a finger across my blue scarf wrapped snuggly around my neck, his look turning serious. "And we might see each other even more."

"Why's that?"

"I've been booking a lot of work because of my mortgage payments."

"You own a house?" I couldn't believe he hadn't

told me about a house. That was major. Yet, I hadn't confessed the magnitude of my debt. He knew I was always short on money since he'd had to float me a few bucks now and then.

He nodded. "It's between my parents' and Dublin. Shauna and I lived there. I couldn't bring myself to sell it after her death. The tenants moved out last year, and it's vacant, so I've been needing extra quid to make the payments. I'm selling it so I won't have to travel as much. Maybe buy a town house with a yard for a dog to run around, like Mr. MacCool."

Was he saying he wanted to live together? I didn't want to rely on Declan for support. I needed to do this on my own. I wanted to spend more time with him, but moving in together would be a major step. I'd been prepared for him to leave stuff at my apartment. To give him a dresser drawer and bathroom counter space. But to *live* together?

He arched a brow. "Right, then, now you're the one acting *freaked* out." He laughed. "I'm not saying we should live together, but it would be nice if you and Mr. MacCool might stay over now and then."

"Even if Matthew McHugh only goes for the contractor position, we'll figure something out. Dublin is just a seven-hour flight from Chicago."

"And I have a shite-load of frequent flyer miles. But you're not going to be needing a backup plan." He glanced down at his finger still resting on my scarf, his smile fading. He raised his gaze, pain in his eyes. "It was a brain aneurysm. She just didn't wake up one morning." He sucked in a ragged breath, then eased it out.

My eyes watered, and I swallowed the lump of emotion in my throat. "I'm so sorry."

"I'm lucky to have the memories. I just need to learn not to hold on to some so fiercely."

I wasn't sure how to respond, since I agreed. It'd taken Declan a long time to open up to me about Shauna. But I also had never experienced and then lost the kind of love he had. I slipped my arms around him, holding him in a tight embrace.

"How about we go practice your pitch?" he said softly.

"Sounds good."

We rode the elevator up, our fingers laced, my head snuggled against Declan's shoulder. He squeezed my hand, his skin warm against mine. We were staring at our hands molded together. He massaged a thumb over my skin, sending tingles up my arm. My breathing quickened, and a light flutter feeling tickled my chest.

We weren't going to my room to practice my pitch.

Yet no gurgling or cramps seized my tummy.

Maybe my previous physical reaction at the thought of making love with Declan had nothing to do with some underlying emotions regarding Andy. Maybe I'd needed Declan to open up more about Shauna. Needed to know that our relationship was moving forward. That it wouldn't revolve around staying in touch via FaceTime while we only saw each other once every two months. Even if I wasn't living in Dublin, Declan would be, and him traveling less would give us more opportunities to see each other. I shouldn't immediately assume emotional issues were related to Andy.

I was moving forward.

We entered my room still holding hands. Declan turned to me with a steamy look that set my body on fire. He placed his hands on the sides of my hips and eased me up against the door. He gently touched his lips to mine. He slid a teasing tongue across my lower lip, then along my upper one before slipping it inside my mouth. After a leisurely kiss, he drew his head back slightly, gazing deep into my eyes, breathing heavily. He slowly unwrapped the scarf draped around my neck and tossed it to the side.

I was going to self-combust! I curled my fingers into his sweater and drew him flush against me, locking lips. Our kiss deepened while we tugged off each other's jackets, letting them fall to the floor. I pulled his sweater up over his head. I fanned my hands across his chest—his broad, incredible chest—then swept them down his arms, over his tattooed bicep. The Celtic symbol for love matched the symbol on his leather bracelet, which he wasn't currently wearing for the first time since we'd met.

His fingers curled around the bottom of my sweater, grazing my bare skin, causing my breath to catch in my throat. I raised my arms over my head, and he peeled it off. He unzipped my jeans and hooked his thumbs around the waistband, slipping the pants down my legs, kneeling in front of me. I stepped from the jeans and stood there in my white lace bra and *Póg Mo Thóin*— Kiss My Ass—undies.

Declan smiled at my undies. "Brilliant idea."

I woke up in the middle of the night, snuggled against Declan's warm, naked body. I placed a hand gently on his chest, feeling the rise and fall of his breathing. As if to make sure this was for real and not merely a dream. I'd never felt such an overwhelming emotional connection to a guy. Or so peaceful, content, happy... It felt right that we'd waited until Ireland. When we were both relaxed and not stressed out by my crazy job.

Our future was here.

Declan stirred, letting out a soft moan. He rolled onto his side, draping an arm across me. I spooned against him, our bodies molded together like our hands had been on the elevator.

"I love you," he whispered, his breath warm against my ear, sending tingles all over my body.

"Love you too."

Part of me wanted to stay awake and savor the moment, but the other part was exhausted and needed to be fresh for my appointment. We'd have tomorrow night together, and many more. In the morning I was going to splurge on room service. Eggs and bacon would replace the romantic dinner I'd had planned in Prague. I smiled, recalling Declan's story about walking in on the room service guy and the keynote speaker covered in the hotel's chocolate soufflé. I closed my eyes. As I drifted back to sleep, I wondered if the Connelly Court Hotel had a signature dessert...

CHAPTER
TWENTY-ONE

I sat on the black leather chair in Flanagan's waiting room, silently practicing my pitch, pretending to read a magazine featuring an article with the brewery's CEO, Matthew McHugh. He was fiftyish, tall, with salt-and-pepper hair. He had on a suit jacket and tie with dark jeans. His relaxed stance and kind smile made him look approachable, unlike his assistant, Gemma, who sat at a black steel-framed desk outside his door. The young woman who'd screwed up Rachel's meetings.

Her blue eyes kept shooting me curious, and suspicious, glances. Did she know Rachel and I were sisters? How hadn't I realized she was the *CEO's* admin? So if I landed the job, I'd have an enemy right off the bat. She'd be my new Gretchen. Everyone's workplace had a Gretchen. However, now that I'd likely never work with Gretchen again, I was growing to tolerate her.

Gemma answered a ringing phone and scribbled on a pad of paper. She hung up and was typing away on her computer when the phone rang again. She put the call on hold while she checked the CEO's schedule on her computer. Maybe she'd be happy to not have to go on-site for meetings. Maybe she constantly screwed up because she didn't have time for it and was trying to do her regular admin duties while working a meeting.

I checked my phone for the dozenth time. Still no text from Rachel. At least her contacting Declan to come here was a step in the right direction. But I still wished that she'd be happier if I got the position than if I didn't.

A photographic history of the brewery lined the wall, including the Brecker integration meeting I'd worked in Dublin last fall. My heart stopped. There was a shot of me dressed in a sausage costume standing between Flanagan's CEO and Brecker's. My blue eyes were visible through the costume's mouth. What if Gemma recognized my eyes? Was that why she kept looking at me? She was trying to place where she'd seen me before? Or maybe she'd already known it was me. Maybe the small type under the photo mentioned my name. When I started working for Flanagan's and took over Gemma's meeting planning duties, she'd tell everyone about me having been a Kildare Sausage.

My breathing quickened. I felt like I was once again suffocating inside the sausage costume!

I peered out the glass doors at employees passing by in the hallway. The elevator just fifty feet away.

"Mr. McHugh will now see you," Gemma said.

I slowly stood. "Thank you."

My gaze darted between the glass doors and the CEO's wooden door—unsure what waited on the other

side. I took a deep, encouraging breath and walked past
her desk, feeling her gaze follow me toward the CEO's
office. I had the feeling she knew who I was but didn't
know why I was there. The sausage picture shouldn't
make me feel embarrassed or ashamed. It should make
me proud of how far I'd come. A lot of people started
out dressed as a sausage. Well, probably not. But
maybe the CEO had started out peddling beers in the
stands at rugby games. Everyone started somewhere.
In only four months, I'd gone from a sausage to a
meeting with the CEO.

I could do this.

❧ ☙

I headed down the sidewalk toward Coffey's pub, my
hand trembling as I disconnected my call with Rachel.
She needed to be the first to know how my meeting had
gone with Matthew McHugh. I didn't want her to hear
about it from the CEO or Gemma. She hadn't reacted
quite as I'd expected. I was still trying to process
exactly how she felt about it.

Heart pounding, I entered the pub. The place had
just opened, so the scent of freshly polished wood
overpowered that of beer and whiskey. Two people sat
at the bar. Declan and Gerry. Declan and I locked
gazes, and the nervous feeling in my chest intensified.
None of us said a word as I walked the length of the
bar.

Declan slipped off his stool, wearing a hesitant
smile, a cautious look in his blue eyes. "Well?"

I slowly smiled. "I'm going to be a Dubliner."

I left out that the job would be a contract position without benefits, yet the CEO had insisted I live in Dublin to be available to go on-site for all meetings, including an upcoming one in Scotland.

I'd worry about that later.

"Brilliant!" Declan wrapped me in a hug and kissed me, filling my mouth with the faint coffee taste of Guinness.

"Fair play to ya." Gerry handed me a pint of cider ale in a logoed Flanagan's glass.

We all raised glasses of my new employer's beer. "*Sláinte.*"

I'd never dreamed that tracing Grandma's ancestry roots would give me the roots I needed to plant myself in Ireland.

The Travel Mishaps of
Caity Shaw

Book 5

Coming
March 2019

AUTHOR'S NOTE

Thank you so much for reading *My Wanderlust Bites the Dust*. If you enjoyed Caity's adventures, I would greatly appreciate you taking the time to leave a review. Reviews encourage potential readers to give my stories a try, and I would love to hear your thoughts.

Thanks a mil!

ABOUT ELIZA WATSON

When Eliza isn't traveling for her job as an event planner, or tracing her ancestry roots through Ireland, she is at home in Wisconsin working on her next novel. She enjoys bouncing ideas off her husband, Mark, and her cats Frankie and Sammy.

Connect with Eliza Online

www.elizawatson.com

www.facebook.com/ElizaWatsonAuthor

www.twitter.com/ElizasBooks

Made in the USA
Coppell, TX
02 May 2021